IN THE HOUSE

OF

ROSEWOOD

IN THE HOUSE OF ROSEWOOD

Book One of *The Rosewood Family Archives*

Ashley Hawley

Edited by Mozelle Jordan.

Cover Illustration by Ashley Hawley.

Paperback ISBN: 979-8-9926659-2-5

eBook ISBN: 979-8-9926659-1-8

Library of Congress Control Number: 2025908218

First Edition: September 2025

North Royalton, Ohio 44133

For content warnings and more information, please visit: ashleyhawley.com.

For Meemaw and GPa.
I'm saving copies for you.

CONTENTS

CHAPTER ONE

Darkness, broken by the familiar image of a glowing white gown that hugs the figure of an unknown woman. Her face is never betrayed, though something in her form strikes a particular chord.

   The woman glides toward a large awning adorned with white roses. Waiting for her beneath the roses is a tall male figure also dressed in white. The man's face is always empty, save for a faint smile. As the woman approaches him, he reaches for her hands. Suddenly, he yanks her toward him, and though the woman wriggles to free herself, the two figures blend into one. A voice from the darkness says, "'Til death do us part." Blood drips over the roses, and the woman's gown turns red. A scream echoes through the void as the figures shrink into the blackness, a pale-blue door locking them away.

Hestia Rosewood sat up in bed, gasping for air. The same dream again. As her breathing returned to its natural rhythm and her eyes adjusted to the darkness, she could just make out the shadows of her bedchamber. The aroma of an English summer night blew in through the open window, and she could hear the subtle sound of crickets chirping. Pulling back the bedsheets, Hestia flung her legs over the side of the bed and tossed her blonde locks behind her shoulders. She sighed as her feet sought the grounding comfort of the cool wooden floor. Even in her short fifteen years, Hestia was no stranger to the occasional nightmare. However, in recent months, this dream had recurred several times, each time taking on a new aspect. This night had her especially perplexed as this was the first time she had heard a voice.

Shaking her head, Hestia noticed a dryness in her throat. She tiptoed toward her bedchamber door and slowly pulled it open, taking care to ensure it did not creak. Though unaccustomed to fetching her own water, Hestia was confident that she could do so without waking the entire manor.

Hestia crossed the threshold into the expansive hallway of Deston Manor. One of the most impressive spectacles in all of Deston, England, the manor had been the birthplace of at least four generations of Rosewood nobility. While, in the light of day, it boasted stunning sconces, the finest artwork, and grand, yet comfortable amenities, Hestia could never shake the foreboding and claustrophobic nature it took on at night. And this night was no different.

As Hestia peered around her, she could scarcely see beyond her nose. Her uncle, August Rosewood, was the present earl of the Rosewood family and had a proclivity for privacy. Despite ongoing warnings around the dangers of stale manor air, August never once allowed the servants to so much as crack an exterior window. In fact, nearly every one was covered by a set of ugly, heavy brown curtains. They blocked out all light, all air, and, in Hestia's opinion, all happiness.

As Hestia shuffled toward the kitchen, she wondered if this was what it felt like to be entombed; you see nothing in front of or behind you, yet you can only move so far. The feeling of being trapped always struck Hestia on the nights she had that dream. It was one of the reasons she enjoyed time in the manor's garden and had begun sleeping with her window open when the weather would permit. She refused to allow her uncle's paranoia to prevent her from tasting the freedom she desperately craved. Even now, her attempt to fetch a glass of water felt as freeing as if she ran toward the manor doors and flung them open, running out into the night.

Just before Hestia reached the threshold of the kitchen, she heard an indistinct noise and turned to find the soft light of a candle floating toward her from the foyer.

"Lady Rosewood?" a soft voice inquired through the candlelight.

As Hestia's eyes adjusted, she finally made out a slim figure and two shining eyes set in a fair, worn face. "Adella?" Hestia said.

"Yes, ma'am," Adella responded nervously, placing a lock of her unkempt black hair behind her ear. "W-what are you doing out of bed?"

"I was just grabbing a glass of water. What are *you* doing out of bed? Did Uncle send you to fetch something?"

August employed an unusually lean staff to manage Deston Manor. There was Jessamine, Hestia's handmaiden and head housemaid, Hiram, the cook, and Adella. Adella was, to Hestia's understanding, hired as a housemaid but one that August kept an intensely watchful eye over. Instead of allowing her to sleep with Jessamine in the servants' quarters that was just off of the kitchen, he made her sleep in a chamber directly across from his. She was barely permitted to even breathe in Hestia's presence, so it was surprising to see her on this night freely wandering about the manor.

"Oh, well, I, uh . . . I was having some trouble sleeping," Adella replied. "We should probably get you back to your room before Lord Rosewood finds you."

Hestia opened her mouth to protest, but as soon as the two turned back around toward the chamber hallway, Hestia's eyes caught a dim glow emanating from August's study at the end of the hall. "Uncle is awake. I could swear those lamps were not lit before."

Adella gripped Hestia's shoulder tightly. "All the more reason for us to get you back to bed. Come along now." Adella rushed the girl back down the hall and into her chamber.

"My water, Adella?" Hestia inquired once she was settled between her sheets.

"Ah, yes, ma'am," Adella said shakily. She crept toward Hestia's door and disappeared behind it.

Moments later, the housemaid returned with a glass of water as Hestia settled herself back in for the night. "There you are," Adella said, handing her the glass. "I should really take my leave now, Lady Rosewood. Good night."

"Adella, have you ever had a recurring dream?" Hestia asked, using this unique opportunity to speak to someone other than her handmaiden about what was troubling her.

"Pardon?"

"What do you think it means when a dream comes to you again and again, revealing more of itself each time but also always leaving you with more questions than answers?"

Adella was silent for a moment, looking Hestia up and down with a face full of curiosity and a hint of concern. "Well, I really don't know," she finally replied. "Perhaps your mind is trying to tell you something that you need to know, but it can't tell you all at once."

"Why not?"

"Our minds have many tremendous abilities, one of which is the ability to protect us. Perhaps your mind cannot tell you everything at once because the pain of the truth may hurt you. Or worse."

The air of Hestia's bedchamber hung thick as Adella's last words rattled inside Hestia's mind.

As if recognizing Hestia's internal strife, Adella suddenly reached out and clutched the young woman's hand. "Lady Rosewood, you should know that—" The words caught in her throat. Shaking her head, she pivoted. "Your uncle intends to hire a new governess for you."

"Oh?" Hestia had not had a governess for nearly five years. Her long-running governess, Ms. Turner, resigned upon the girl's tenth birthday. She assumed, as most would, that Hestia would now either prepare to enter society and become a wife or further her education with August. However, August did not possess the time or patience to provide Hestia with any lessons himself, nor did he appear keen on introducing her to anything or anyone beyond the walls of Deston Manor. It was surprising that he would be willing to pay for a governess now and could find one willing to teach a girl as old as Hestia.

"I know that your history with governesses has been a bit . . . rocky," Adella said.

Hestia snorted. "That's putting it mildly." Despite Hestia's interest in education, she never possessed the proper spirit for the gentler subjects a lady was meant to be taught. She often desired to push beyond those boundaries, much to her governess' chagrin. Hestia could still recall Ms. Turner's parting words to her uncle: *That girl shall never make a proper bride until that wild spirit of hers is tempered.* It was a statement that filled Hestia with a secret pride to this day.

"But I would suggest you listen to this new one," Adella said. "She may teach you more than you expect." Adella tightly gripped the girl's hands.

Hestia, in shock at this sudden act of intimacy, silently nodded.

"Good," Adella said, loosening her hands. "Well, I suppose we all should be back to bed now." With that, the housemaid turned and headed for the door.

As Hestia turned over, she heard Adella's voice once more. "Lady Rosewood?"

"Yes, Adella?"

"I am sorry if your recurring dream brings you distress."

"It's quite alright, Adella. I will be fine."

Adella flashed Hestia a small smile and closed the door to her chamber behind her, leaving Hestia in the darkness once again.

"I know you will," the housemaid whispered as she leaned against the door. No more than a few seconds after she moved to return to her quarters, a cold hand fell upon her shoulder.

"Adella," a deep voice said. "Please come to my study."

CHAPTER TWO

The next morning, Hestia stood in her bedchamber wearing nothing but a shift and rubbed a washcloth along her forearms, divulging Adella's report about the new governess to her handmaiden. Jessamine was a short, plump older woman who had raised Hestia from her toddler years. Ever efficient, she had already fixed Hestia's bedsheets, pulled out her dress, and changed her water once before the young woman had even finished cleaning the left half of her body.

"And you said you heard this from Adella?" Jessamine questioned, standing by as Hestia hiked up her shift to wash her legs.

"Yes."

"I just hope Lord Rosewood doesn't catch wind of you two speaking." Jessamine spent much time with Adella during the day and knew of August's reluctance to allow her to be near Hestia. The reason for this was lost even on her; but ever the faithful servant, she made every effort to ensure this was upheld when and where she was present.

"He'll never find out if nobody tells him." Hestia shot Jessamine a knowing look. As much as she loved Jessamine, she could never quite understand the handmaiden's staunch loyalty to her uncle. She was always the first one to defend him, reminding Hestia that he is the one "caring for her" and "ensuring her success in life." Never mind the fact that he kept her confined to the manor twenty-four seven, with little outside influence, save for her daily trips to the garden.

"Hestia!" Jessamine exclaimed. "Now, I know you are not telling me to lie to Lord Rosewood."

"Of course not, Jessamine," Hestia replied. "I am only asking you to pretend as if you did not hear my story." The girl interlaced both hands and tucked them under her chin, batting her lashes at the handmaiden.

Jessamine looked at the girl for a moment before letting out a sigh. "Oh, alright." As much as Jessamine valued August's employment, she valued her relationship with Hestia just a little bit more.

"Thank you, Jessamine!"

The handmaiden set Hestia's washbowl aside and handed her a dry towel.

"Well, that wasn't all that happened last night, Jessamine. I also had that dream again. And this time, there was a woman's voice. She sounded so . . . scared. It was horrible."

"I've told you those books you read are putting fantastic things into your head," Jessamine replied as she grabbed Hestia's petticoats. "A lady your age really should be reading gentler things."

Books were one of Hestia's few reprieves from the isolated life August had cultivated for her. Her uncle possessed a large wooden bookcase in his study that was half covered by a thick damask sheet. He permitted her to sample any uncovered works as she wished, which, over the years, she eagerly devoured. "Jessamine, I read those stories *because* they are so fantastic. They excite me far more than all of this." Hestia waved her hand about the chamber, dropping her towel.

"Now, you best not let Lord Rosewood hear you speaking in such a way," Jessamine said, leaning down to grab the towel. "He's done a—"

"Great sacrifice raising you for all of these years," both women spoke the line verbatim.

"I know, Jessamine," Hestia said. "I just wish that *his* sacrifice did not limit *me* so much."

As Jessamine gathered the first layer of Hestia's clothing, they heard a light rapping at the door.

"Oh, I wonder who that could—"

Before Jessamine finished her thought, Hestia had pulled on one of her morning robes and raced to the door. "Yes?" she said as she swung the door open.

A young man, not much older than she, looked up at Hestia with gray eyes. He was dressed in slacks and an undershirt, both covered in what appeared to be dirt. His dark blond locks lay a bit disheveled on his head. His freckled cheeks turned pink as he noticed Hestia's presence. "My apologies, my lady. I was l-looking for Lord Rosewood, and she p-pointed at this door." The boy gestured behind him.

Hestia saw Adella mutely standing by. She nodded in the girl's direction before disappearing down the hall. Hestia's eyes followed her until she was out of sight, brows furrowed.

"I apologize, ma'am," the young man repeated. "I certainly did not expect to address the lady of the house."

Hestia beamed at being referred to in such a way. "That's quite alright, Mr.—"

"Miller, ma'am. Ezekiel Miller." Ezekiel bowed.

"We have a gardener by the name of Miller. Are you a relation?"

"Yes, ma'am. He is my father."

Ambrose Miller had worked as the Rosewood's gardener since before Hestia was born. He was a kind man but a noted recluse, never venturing far beyond the garden or his own cottage. Hestia had eavesdropped on enough of her uncle's conversations to hear rumors that he'd once been married, until he discovered that his wife had an affair and threw her out. The last Hestia heard was that she had passed away, but the girl never would have thought that mess had bore a child.

"Oh, I did not know that Mr. Miller had a son," Hestia said.

"Yes, well, before my mother, before she passed, she sent me back to live with my father. So, I am here now and ready to help him. That's actually why I came inside the manor. I was waiting outside while my father speaks with Lord Rosewood, but I remembered that we have to go into town to pick up supplies from a merchant who's closing soon. I came in to fetch him, but I seem to have gotten lost."

"Well, why don't I help you out then," Jessamine intervened, pushing past Hestia at the chamber doorway. "I suspect they're in the study just down the hall." Jessamine wrapped an arm around Ezekiel's shoulder and turned him around.

"I take many walks through the garden, so I do look forward to seeing you again, Ezekiel," Hestia said just as Jessamine began ushering him away.

Ezekiel paused mid-step, causing Jessamine to falter in her stride, and faced Hestia once more. "It would be an honor, ma'am," Ezekiel noted with another quick bow.

"You may call me—" The words caught in Hestia's throat as she noticed a large figure approaching Jessamine and Ezekiel from behind.

"What is the meaning of this?" August's booming voice caused both Jessamine and Ezekiel to jump. They spun to face the lord of the manor. August was a tall, lean man. He dressed in all black, and his graying hair, while well-groomed, always appeared a bit greasy. The dull, pallid skin of his face held a few wrinkles to betray his age. A striking feature of his, however, were his eyes. Such piercing eyes, the color of rolling smog. They could nearly burn a hole straight through one's soul. And at this moment, those two daggers settled directly on Hestia.

"Lord," Jessamine said with a bow. "My apologies. I thought you would be in your study."

"I was," August stated matter-of-factly before breaking eye contact with Hestia and looking Ezekiel up and down. "You must be Ambrose's son. He has told me all about you. Seems your mother never shared that she was with child during her *unfortunate* separation from your father."

"Yes, sir," Ezekiel said, cheeks turning red again.

Hestia saw the corner of August's mouth twitch, as if fighting the urge to grin at Ezekiel's discomfort.

"I am here now because my mother is not with us anymore. It was either this or the workhouse."

"Well, I have given your father permission to allow you on the grounds. But mark me, boy . . ." August leaned closer to Ezekiel. "You take one step out of line, and the workhouse will be calling for you and your father both."

"Yes, sir," Ezekiel said, a slight shiver in his voice.

August continued to dig his eyes into Ezekiel's for several seconds before looking back to Jessamine. "Jessamine, take the boy to fetch his father from my study. Then, return and ensure that my niece finishes dressing." August glanced at Hestia with obvious annoyance.

"Yes, Lord Rosewood," Jessamine said, hurrying Ezekiel down the hall.

"Uncle," Hestia began. "I—"

"Hestia, you live under my roof, do you not?"

"Yes, Uncle."

"And while under my roof, you are to behave in the manner befitting a noble lady."

"Uncle, Ezekiel was just—"

"Hestia, your conduct reflects the very essence of Deston Manor. For you to be conversing so casually with a young member of the opposite sex in no more than a dressing gown . . . If I had been entertaining a guest, an act such as that would have besmirched our name."

"With all due respect, Uncle," Hestia retorted. "I hardly think it is more becoming of a lady of the house to ignore a knock at her door."

August's gaze softened. He reached out and cradled Hestia's chin with his thumb and forefinger. "So much of your mother I see in you."

Hestia froze as she felt his icy fingers caress her delicate skin.

August's eyes darkened before blinking back to their natural state, his hand dropping from Hestia's face to his side. "You still have far to go before you are fit to bear the moniker of a lady of the house, my dear niece. A first step in that process will be to learn how to follow directions. When Jessamine returns, she will finish getting you dressed. Have her bring you to my study once you are decent. We have something to discuss."

Twenty minutes later, powdered, hair brushed, and tied into her corset and petticoats, Hestia exited her chamber and made her way down the hall. The walls of Deston Manor bore portraits of all descendants of the noble Rosewood family. As she passed the stern visage of her grandfather, Thaddeus Rosewood, Hestia imagined what the man had been like. He, like her mother and father, had died before her memory could serve her, leaving only August and herself to carry on the Rosewood bloodline. She rarely dared to gaze at his portrait for fear that those eyes would draw her into an inescapable madness.

The final portrait before her uncle's study depicted the softer visages of a man and a woman. The man was formal, yet friendly, and the woman was fair, blonde, and had warm green eyes much like her own. They were Jonathan and Helena Rosewood, Hestia's parents.

Hestia knew very little about the specific fate that befell her parents, though she had pressed her uncle for more information on multiple occasions. She only ceased her questioning when, about a year ago, August flew into a rage and sent her to her chamber without supper. So, Hestia would stare at the portrait, willing it to come alive and lay bare its knowledge. Even a narrative invented by her own mind would serve her better than none at all.

Once Hestia entered her uncle's study, he pointed to the empty seat in front of him. "Have a seat." August sighed. "Tomorrow, I will be going away on business. I shall not return for at least a fortnight, but it may be longer if purpose serves."

Hestia kept her face still as stone to resist betraying her excitement. August, a creature of habit, was never gone from the manor longer than a week at a time. Now, he would be gone for at least two.

"During this time, you will have the opportunity to earn the moniker you so boldly claim as lady of the house. I shall leave your daily care to Jessamine, Adella will maintain the upkeep of the manor, and Hiram will be at your service for meals, of course. I have also employed a new governess who will ensure that you are brushed up on your education."

Hestia feigned a look of surprise. "I thought my education was to cease following Ms. Turner's resignation?"

"Yes, well, I have been thinking about it, and now that you are older, there are some duties that you will be expected to take on as a member of the Rosewood lineage. Therefore, it is prudent that you receive some additional education that Ms. Turner did not provide."

"Who should I have the pleasure of making the acquaintance of, Uncle?"

"Her name is Ms. Priscilla Evans, and she comes highly regarded from one of London's best workhouses."

"When does she come?"

"You will make her acquaintance here, in my study, at precisely noon tomorrow. You two will have a chance to meet and hear my expectations for your education before I take my leave." August rose from his chair and motioned for Hestia to do the same. "I suppose you should run along to your breakfast now, my dear niece." He led Hestia to the door and watched as she walked down the hall.

Uncle will be gone for two weeks! The thought bounced excitedly inside of Hestia's mind. *Perhaps this will finally be my chance to uncover his secrets.* While August relented access to a few main areas of Deston Manor, there were others strictly prohibited to her view. A thrill went through Hestia at the prospect of what stories lie in wait. She considered the possibility of pulling back the damask sheet that covered half of the large bookcase in his study, revealing his hidden tomes to the world. *Or maybe I will finally explore the second floor.* The second story of Deston Manor was a particular mystery to Hestia, as she was never allowed to venture anywhere near it. When questioning her uncle on his reluctance, he had only provided a vague clue: "The walls of this manor hold many great tales, but some are better left forgotten."

For many years, Hestia had obeyed her uncle's warning and kept those beastly stories at bay. But this was her chance to finally awaken those beasts from their slumber.

CHAPTER THREE

The next day, as the manor clocks struck 11:59 a.m., Hestia approached her uncle's study and rapped on the door.

"My dear niece, please come in," August said.

Hestia entered the room and took note of the stranger across from her uncle's desk. She was thin and held an old brown suitcase. Despite her youthful complexion, a few wrinkles confirmed the hardships she must have faced while in the workhouse. Hestia knew very little about the state of London's workhouses, though she did understand that they were quite cramped and unsanitary, certainly a far cry from the life she lived, as oppressive as it may feel to her. Hestia could already hear Jessamine chirping in her ear, reminding her to be grateful for what her uncle has given her, for many, like Ms. Evans, did not have such luxurious options.

Ms. Evans had her brunette hair in a tight bun, though some strands had broken free. She wore a simple dress, wrinkled, but nicer than Hestia would have expected. As the young girl scanned her new governess, she arrived back at the face and was met with two large brown eyes. These eyes were traditionally unremarkable; a bit sunken, as if sleep had evaded the poor woman for years. So, Hestia was surprised to see them wide and boring straight into her own, almost in a state of shock.

"Hestia," August began. "Please meet the acquaintance of Ms. Priscilla Evans, your new governess."

Hestia recalled when Adella implored her to listen to this new governess. *What could she possibly have to teach me?* Hestia wondered. Nevertheless, Hestia gave a small curtsey and addressed the woman directly. "Ms. Evans, it is a pleasure to meet my new governess. I very much look forward to our lessons together."

Priscilla said nothing at first, her eyes scanning Hestia up and down. But then suddenly, as if snapping herself back from a dream, Priscilla shook her head and set the suitcase down beside her. "Y-yes," she said. "I do look forward to working with you as well." Priscilla gave a small nod of her head.

"You two will be closely linked these next two weeks—" August began.

"And hopefully longer," Priscilla interjected. "Given, of course, that Lady Rosewood's imagination does not get the better of her, as you mentioned, Lord Rosewood."

I see Uncle is already coloring her opinion, Hestia thought.

"Yes," August said. "That is why I wanted to have this meeting before I left, to ensure that all are of equal understanding as to my wishes and expectations while I am away."

For the better part of the next hour, August provided Hestia and Priscilla with the list of his expectations for Hestia's education. As he spoke, Hestia could feel each time that Priscilla's eyes darted in her direction, boring into the side of her skull. When the clock struck one, August called for Jessamine to round up the remaining manor staff for an overview of his expectations while he was away.

As August talked with the gardener, Ambrose Miller, Hestia stole a few glances at his son. She had not had the opportunity to see him clean, but now she really noticed his freckled cheeks and striking eyes, which cast more than a few glimpses in her direction, only to look back down when they met her own eyes.

At last, the time had come for August's departure. Both Hestia and Priscilla followed him to the door. "Take good care, Uncle," Hestia said, keeping her voice even.

August took up Hestia's slender wrist and kissed the top of her hand. "My dear niece."

Hestia uncomfortably smiled before pulling away. She then stealthily wiped her hand across the back of her dress, only stopping when she noticed Priscilla eyeing her once more.

"I expect to see a properly educated lady once I return," August addressed Priscilla.

Priscilla nodded. "I can assure you, Lord Rosewood, upon your return, Lady Rosewood will have more knowledge than you could scarcely imagine."

Both women watched as August's carriage clattered along the cobblestones and into the afternoon sun. Once the carriage was out of sight, they returned to the house. Hestia caught sight of Ezekiel back in the garden and waved.

He smiled and bowed in return.

"Lady Rosewood," Jessamine greeted her at the door. "It's time for your afternoon tea."

"Very good, Jessamine. Ms. Evans, I expect our lessons are to begin tomorrow morning, to give you time to settle in." Hestia turned to follow Jessamine to the kitchen.

"Well," Priscilla began. "I was actually hoping to begin at least one lesson this afternoon. We could start after your tea, of course."

Hestia grinned and turned around, ready to test her boundaries. "Oh, Ms. Evans," she began in a distressed voice she reserved for inconveniences. "I am not sure today would be at all a useful time to start, for I am much too exhausted. I dare say I would not pay adequate attention. Perhaps tomorrow morning—"

"You are not often left alone, are you, Lady Rosewood?" Priscilla said.

"Pardon?"

"Forgive me, but it seems as if this false show of exhaustion is an attempt to test my willingness to allow you to shirk the activities in which your uncle wishes you to participate in."

The girl was unsure whether she should be nervous or impressed that Priscilla had found her out so quickly.

"Is this because we are now without the presence of your uncle? Or do you act in this manner with all governesses?"

Hestia opened her mouth to respond, but Priscilla opened hers first. "I would imagine this defiant streak would be deemed unacceptable to August, so you must display it outside of his presence. And now that he is gone for two weeks, you feel a sense of liberation that you have not felt for quite some time. Or perhaps ever." Priscilla stepped closer to Hestia, who gulped. "Your uncle, he makes you uneasy."

Hestia's eyes widened.

"It was not difficult to see in the short time he was here with you. Your countenance changed dramatically as soon as that door shut, and once you knew your uncle was no longer in this manor, you relaxed. Not to mention how you quite literally rubbed his affection off onto your skirt."

"You . . . saw that?"

Priscilla nodded with a chuckle.

"I must apologize, though, Lady Rosewood. I believe that I may have put you off upon our first meeting by staring at you so boldly. It is just that you remind me so much of . . . of someone who I used to know. But I would very much like it if I could become a friend to you, as well as a teacher. In fact, I believe that we both have much to learn from each other."

Hestia turned to Jessamine, who was suspiciously eyeing Priscilla. She turned back to the governess with a nervous smile. "I—I would like that as well, Ms. Evans," Hestia said.

Priscilla smiled before dropping into a more authoritative stance. "However, we cannot expect to learn from each other if you are intent on denying me the opportunity to get to know you. So, I will expect two things from you for each of our sessions together. First, punctuality. Unless you are feeling ill or otherwise incapacitated, I will ask that you arrive at our sessions on time.

Second, truth. If I am to guide you, I will require openness and honesty at all times. Am I clear?"

"Yes, Ms. Evans."

"Good. Well, I suppose it would be helpful for me to settle in for the day and get my bearings of the manor before we begin our lessons. So, you will get your wish this once, Lady Rosewood. But I expect to see you in the drawing room by no later than 8:00 a.m. tomorrow morning. Is that acceptable?"

"Yes, Ms. Evans," Hestia repeated.

Suddenly, Adella raced up to Priscilla and handed her the suitcase she had left in August's study. Surprised she had forgotten it, Priscilla took the case and turned to look at Adella, who merely gave a small curtsey before fleeing.

Priscilla then looked at Jessamine. "Jessamine, please excuse my delay. You may now escort Lady Rosewood to her afternoon tea."

Hestia and Jessamine headed toward the kitchen as Priscilla retired to her quarters. The pair walked silently, the only sound being the echo of their feet upon the wooden floor.

He makes you uneasy. The phrase rattled in Hestia's mind. For someone who had just arrived at the manor that day, Priscilla already seemed to have a stronger grasp of Hestia's relationship with her uncle than even herself. Hestia had certainly never met a governess with as much intuitive prowess as this woman had displayed thus far.

Hestia was grateful to see that the rest of the day was quite uneventful. As day turned into night, Jessamine dressed her in her bedclothes, turned down her bed, and took her leave, allowing Hestia to fall into a troubled, but deep, sleep.

———— ❧ ————

A sweeping white gown. A tall male figure. Both illuminated brightly in the darkness. They smile at each other, though the rest of their faces cannot be made out. He reaches for her hands. She hesitates, seeing his hands are spattered with blood. He grips her wrists, and she struggles to free herself. She cries out, but no sound can be heard. A male voice whispers, "'Til death do us part." The scene panes outward as a pale-blue door shuts the figures away. A female voice screams, "What have you done? No! No! No! No, no, no . . ."

Hestia awoke, her eyes adjusting to the darkness. Her heart pounded nearly out of her chest so rapidly that she hardly noticed a disembodied voice echoing "no" until she calmed herself. As her heart returned to its natural pace, she realized that the voice that woke her was still there, waiting in the hallway outside of her door.

"No, no, no," the voice bellowed.

Hestia slowly got out of her bed and inched toward the door of her bedchamber. She cracked it open, the old wood creaking. Hestia poked her head out and peered into the darkness. As she looked right, she squinted, making out a slender figure gliding toward her uncle's study. Hestia froze in fear. *Am I still dreaming?*

"No, no, no," the voice said, as the figure continued making its way down the hall. At last, it paused in front of the portraits outside of August's study.

Hestia opened her door wider and crept out into the dark hallway. The hair on her arms stood up as she tiptoed down the hall toward the figure. When she was close enough, Hestia called into the darkness. "H-hello?"

There was no response, save for the whispered cries of, "No, no, no."

Hestia's fear rose with each step, but so did her curiosity. She had read and heard of spectres who visit unsuspecting individuals in the night, though she hardly ever expected that she may be one of those poor souls. Finally, Hestia was within arm's length of the figure whose back faced her. Against her better judgment, Hestia reached her arm out, but just before she could make contact with the spectre, it turned to face her. Hestia gasped, for this was no spectre at all, but Ms. Priscilla Evans. Her eyes were closed and her face appeared scrunched, as if in pain. "Ms. Evans," Hestia began, confused. "Wh-what are you doing here?"

Priscilla's sunken eyes shot wide open, her brows nearly touching her hairline. Her face depicted the very essence of fear. She opened her mouth and shouted, "Helena!" Suddenly, Priscilla crumpled and fell to the ground.

Hestia stood in shock for a moment before tapping her on the back. "Ms. Evans, are you alright? Ms. Evans!" When Priscilla didn't move, Hestia shook her until she finally awoke, frantically peering into the blackness.

"Wh-where am I?" Priscilla softly cried.

"It is alright, Ms. Evans," Hestia said, helping her to her feet. "You are still in Deston Manor, just outside of my uncle's study."

Priscilla looked toward the closed door of August's study and then saw the portrait of Hestia's parents in front of her. She turned to look at Hestia, confusion and fear tingeing her features.

"Ms. Evans, why—"

"Dearie, what are you doing out of bed?"

Both women jumped at hearing the unexpected voice. Jessamine stood in the hall holding a dimly-lit oil lamp. She squinted until she noticed both Hestia and Priscilla in the hall together. "Oh, Ms. Evans. I didn't expect to see you here with Lady Rosewood."

"I just woke up to . . . get a glass of water and saw Ms. Evans looking . . . for the kitchen," Hestia lied.

Priscilla looked at Hestia with appreciation before continuing the charade. "Yes, and I apologize if I disturbed either of you. I suppose I still need to grow accustomed to the manor's layout."

"That's fine, Ms. Evans . . . I just noticed that your quarters were empty, so I came to see if everything was alright."

"Everything's fine, Jessamine," Hestia replied, Priscilla nodding in agreement.

"Well, head on back to your chamber, dearie," Jessamine said. "I will fetch your water and take Ms. Evans to the kitchen."

"Thank you, Jessamine. Ms. Evans." Hestia curtsied at the governess and returned to her chambers. As she crawled back into bed, her mind was reeling. The image of Priscilla's eyes, wide in horror, burned into her memory. Many questions plagued the young girl's mind as she waited for Jessamine to return with the glass of water she did not need. However, one thought rose high above the rest: *Why, of all words, did Ms. Evans shout my mother's name?*

CHAPTER FOUR

As the morning sun cascaded over Deston Manor, Hestia could think of nothing more than the strange events that had transpired the night before. The terror on Priscilla's face invaded her memory, though not nearly as much as the name she had shouted. The coincidental manner of her shouting the name of Hestia's mother, while standing in front of her parents' portrait, gave doubt just enough permission to begin tiptoeing across the threshold of her thoughts. These wonderings continued as Jessamine assisted in dressing her for the morning.

"Are you alright, dearie?" The handmaiden questioned.

"Huh?" Hestia began. "Oh, yes, Jessamine. I am fine."

"You're just so quiet this morning. Did something happen last night with Ms. Evans?"

In that moment, something inside of Hestia told her to remain aloof. "No, nothing with Ms. Evans, Jessamine. I just . . . didn't sleep well."

This seemed to satisfy the handmaiden for the time, as she finished dressing Hestia and escorted her to the drawing room. Priscilla Evans stood in the room by one of the side tables, sorting through a collection of books and parchments. Jessamine announced Hestia's presence.

"Ah, Lady Rosewood, right on time." Priscilla said. "Thank you, Jessamine."

The handmaiden took her leave, allowing the two women to get started.

They stood awkwardly for a moment before Priscilla motioned for Hestia to take a seat beside her. "Well," Priscilla began.

Hestia could feel the tension in the air.

"I suppose we should dive into our lesson for the day, Lady Rosewood."

"You may call me Hestia, Ms. Evans."

"Thank you . . . *Hestia*."

"You are welcome, Ms. Evans. I have endeavored for years now to persuade Jessamine to call me the same. She does often call me 'dearie,' but feels it is best that we 'maintain a more formal relationship in the presence of new or noble company.'"

"Well, I am by no means noble company," Priscilla said. "And I request no special treatment as a new member of the household. Though, I admire your handmaiden's formality."

"Yes, but rest assured, no formality is required around me, Ms. Evans. After all, if we are to become friends, as you suggested yesterday, there is no need to maintain formalities. We cannot expect to become friends if openness and truth are not at the forefront of our relationship. Isn't that right?"

Priscilla nodded, and Hestia was sure she heard her gulp.

"I suppose before we begin our lesson today, it may be prudent to clear the air. Upon our first meeting, I noted that I expected truth from our relationship. Last night—"

Hestia held her breath, as if awaiting a confession or grand reveal.

"Last night, I put you in a position where you felt you had to lie to your handmaiden. I apologize for that and wanted to assure you that it will not happen again. Despite what you may learn about me, Hestia, I *do* value honesty. For now, I would very much appreciate it if we can put the past behind us and move forward with today's first lesson." Without waiting to hear Hestia's response, Priscilla pulled out a few books and began preparing her notes for their lesson.

Even with the gesture to put last night's events behind them, Hestia still felt the weight of the sleepwalking incident burdening the room with a thick aura.

Priscilla saw Hestia give her a curious look and returned one of nervousness and a hint of pleading. Her eyes spoke to Hestia directly, as if to say "all you want to know will be answered, but please not here, and please not now."

Hestia wasn't known for holding her tongue but felt she should at this moment.

Over the next several hours, Ms. Evans trained Hestia on the softer arts of academia. Hestia took so particularly well to her lessons in French that she found herself begging Ms. Evans to teach her one more phrase before the end of their lesson.

"Very well," Ms. Evans stated. She flipped through the book until she came upon the word she desired. She turned the book to face Hestia and pointed to the word with a slender finger.

"*Menteur*," Hestia read aloud.

"Would you like to guess the translation?"

Hestia pondered for a moment. "Hmm, it sounds similar to 'mentor.' Is it some variation of the term?"

"It means 'liar,'" Ms. Evans stated matter-of-factly.

Hestia rolled her head up to face Ms. Evans.

"Sometimes, those who are meant to protect and guide us in this world harbor dark secrets. Sometimes, they lie and deceive. These individuals are far more dangerous than they appear, but fate often has a way of pulling the curtain on their charades." Hestia and Priscilla watched each other for a moment before Priscilla closed the book and stood up. "I suppose that is enough for today. It is nearly noon and almost time for your lunch."

As Priscilla put her teaching items away, Hestia decided to test the waters once again. If the governess wouldn't share more from the night's events, perhaps she would share more on other parts of her life. "Ms. Evans, what was it like, living in a workhouse?"

Ms. Evans stopped in her tracks, turning to face Hestia.

"My uncle mentioned that you came from one of the local workhouses," Hestia said.

Priscilla set her book down, but did not acknowledge that the girl had spoken otherwise.

"Forgive me, Ms. Evans. I know very little of the quality of life those who live in workhouses possess."

"It is quite alright, Hestia. It was not what I would exactly call a 'quality of life' at all. The rooms were crowded, the conditions were dirty, and the food was poor. But they sustained me from the time I turned nineteen years old. Of course, when this position promised much better accommodations, I jumped at the opportunity."

"What led you to enter the workhouse?"

"Well, I have never been married, and my parents passed away when I was eighteen. I was alone and needed food, shelter, and money. The working class have so few options as it is, and even fewer opportunities exist for women. So, I took what I could find."

"Oh," Hestia replied.

"It wasn't all bad, though. I did become acquainted with another woman while I was there. She was quite dear to me, in fact, until she passed not too long ago."

"Who was she?"

Priscilla opened her mouth when, suddenly, Jessamine appeared through the drawing room entrance.

"Lady Rosewood, it is time for lunch."

"Ah, perfect timing," Priscilla said. "We have just completed today's lesson, and I am feeling a bit tired, so I think it is time I take my noon rest." Disregarding the fact that the two had been mid-conversation, Priscilla began gathering her things, saying nothing more to Hestia. "Jessamine, would you mind if I had a word with you before you take Lady Rosewood to lunch?"

Jessamine's eyes darted toward Hestia before she responded. "Of course, Ms. Evans. Lady Rosewood, would you mind waiting here a moment?"

Hestia nodded and remained seated in the drawing room as the two stepped into the hallway.

After a few minutes, Priscilla left and Jessamine returned, ushering Hestia to follow her down the hall.

"What did she want, Jessamine?" Hestia inquired.

"She just wanted to know a bit more about you, dearie," Jessamine replied. "Don't worry, I didn't tell her more than she needs to know. Did you enjoy your first session with her?"

"It was . . . interesting. I suspect that Ms. Evans and I have a great deal to learn from each other."

"Well, that's good, dearie," Jessamine said.

As Hestia and Jessamine headed toward the dining room, Hestia peeked behind one of the curtains to see out of the window. "Ooh, Jessamine, it is such a beautiful day today. I would quite like to take my lunch in the garden, and perhaps, have a walk afterward."

Jessamine sighed and took a look out the window herself. "I suppose I can talk to Hiram and get everything set up outside."

Hestia clapped in glee as Jessamine headed to the kitchen to speak with the cook.

Hestia sat in the garden of Deston Manor, her latest well-worn read balanced in her lap as she nibbled some buttered bread and sipped her tea in the rare English sunshine. She watched the bees flitter between the roses, burying beneath the petals to uncover their treasures. She heard the calls of birds and felt the warmth of summer envelope her. Jessamine and Adella were tending to housework, Hiram was cleaning the kitchen, and her uncle was miles away. Hestia greatly enjoyed her time alone. No one else existed in those moments except herself and the characters that lay within the pages she so adored.

As Hestia looked out across the garden's vast expanse, she caught movement out of the corner of her eye. She turned and saw Ezekiel tending to some shrubbery. He seemed to notice her as well and nodded in her direction.

Hestia rose from her seat, placed her book upon the table, and glided to him. "Good afternoon, Ezekiel."

"Lady Rosewood," Ezekiel replied with a bow.

"The shrubs are looking quite healthy this summer."

"Thank you, ma'am."

"You may call me Hestia."

"My apologies ma—Hestia," Ezekiel corrected.

"I had meant to tell you that upon our first meeting, before my uncle intervened."

"Yes, Lord Rosewood is quite an . . . intimidating man."

"Yes, well, that is certainly putting it politely," Hestia said. "I am sorry if he made you feel uncomfortable."

"That's alright. My father had warned me a bit about the Lord's ways."

"As someone who has lived with him for fifteen years, please do not think me wicked for saying that I am most pleased to be rid of him for a while."

Ezekiel smiled. "If you don't mind me asking, how *are* you getting along in that large house by yourself?"

"I would hardly say that I am alone. There is Adella, Hiram, and Jessamine—" Hestia paused before continuing. "And my new governess."

Ezekiel caught the change in Hestia's voice. "Is she not agreeable to you?"

"No, no, she's fine," Hestia replied. "She's just . . . unusual."

"Unusual?"

Hestia wondered if she should continue. After all, she didn't know this young man very well and couldn't guarantee that anything she said wouldn't get back to the wrong person. However, as she looked into Ezekiel's eyes, something inside told her she could trust him. "When we first met, she stared at me quite intently. She claimed I reminded her of someone she knew, but she didn't elaborate further."

"That doesn't sound *too* odd," Ezekiel said.

"That's not all. Last night, I was awoken by a wailing in the hall outside of my chamber. When I opened the door, I saw Ms. Evans. I believe she was sleepwalking. She kept repeating the word 'no, no, no' until at last, she stopped in front of the portrait of my parents and she . . . she cried out my deceased mother's name."

"I didn't know your mother had passed," Ezekiel said. "I'm sorry."

"Thank you, Ezekiel. Both of my parents have been gone since I was three years old, so I do not remember much about them."

"Did you ask Ms. Evans about the situation?"

"She skirted around the subject this morning, but if she knows something about my family, I should think I have the right to inquire. Even if it is something she feels she needs to keep from me."

"I suppose I would agree. I couldn't imagine not knowing everything about my mother and father."

Hestia looked toward the manor, holding those places she had yet to traverse. "I have known for years that Uncle has been keeping secrets from me. I highly suspect that Ms. Evans has secrets, too. Secrets that she wants to tell me but is . . . afraid to."

"Afraid?"

Hestia continued to gaze at the manor, contemplating.

"Well," Ezekiel said, breaking the awkward silence. "I am sure she will tell you what she wants you to know when the time is right."

Another beat of silence fell between them before Hestia let out a whispered thought. "Unless I force those secrets into the light."

"Pardon?"

"If Ms. Evans refuses to tell me what she is hiding, then perhaps I should investigate for myself. She came to us carrying a large brown suitcase. Maybe it holds some documents or photos that could reveal the truth. If only I could access it." Hestia thought for a moment. "Lunch is the only time of day when Jessamine usually leaves me be, especially if I make the rare decision to eat outside. But if I am careful, I could sneak back into the manor, conduct my investigation, and return to my spot in the garden before she returns to fetch me for the afternoon."

"Hestia, if you don't mind me asking, how are you planning to investigate Ms. Evans while she is in the manor with you?"

"Ms. Evans said that she was lying down for her noon rest today. If that is a daily occurrence, I would just have to time it right and stealthily explore her belongings while she is asleep."

"Forgive me, Hestia, but this plan of yours sounds rather risky. Even if you could get into where Ms. Evans is sleeping, your skirts would most likely give you away."

"That's true," Hestia said. She pondered this for a moment until her eyes flashed with inspiration. "Ezekiel, how adept are you at stealth?"

Ezekiel offered Hestia a confused expression in response.

"Do you feel you could move about undetected in relative silence?"

"Well, I've never had much of a chance to practice such a thing, but I suppose so. Why?"

"I know that you and I do not know each other well, and what I am about to ask of you will require the utmost risk and trust, but I cannot accomplish this task alone." She placed a hand upon Ezekiel's shoulder, an action that made the young man's ears flush.

Despite his trepidation, he heard himself blurt out, "What do you need from me?"

Hestia clapped her hands together like a giddy schoolgirl. "Oh, thank you, Ezekiel." She wrapped her arms around him. He returned the hug tentatively, feeling his heart rate increase as her grip tightened. The pair pulled away quickly and began discussing the plan of attack.

"It is far too late to pull this off today, but what is your schedule for tomorrow? Can you be in this same location at this same time tomorrow afternoon?"

"Tomorrow? So soon?"

"The sooner, the better," Hestia said. "After all, Uncle will only be gone for so long. We are on borrowed time as it is."

"Then, I suppose I will be here tomorrow."

"Excellent!" Hestia said.

"But I will need to be back in the garden within an hour. My father comes out to check on me then."

"That should not be a problem. I will have to come back out myself to ensure I am at the table when Jessamine returns."

With that, they shook hands and parted for the rest of the day, the plans replaying in both of their heads.

As Hestia and Ezekiel returned to their responsibilities, Priscilla Evans sat on the bed in her sleeping quarters inside Deston Manor. In her hand, she held a yellowed photograph that she had retrieved from under her pillow. In it, one young girl with dark hair had her head turned away from the camera. Another, with light hair, smiled boldly at the lens. Priscilla stroked the photo gingerly as tears formed in her eyes. "I found her," Priscilla said, her voice cracking. "I know I couldn't save you, but I *will* save her."

CHAPTER FIVE

Each step of Hestia's plan replayed itself in Ezekiel's mind as he watched the sun's rays lightly kiss the stone walls of Deston Manor from the window of the cottage he and his father occupied. His stomach fluttered at the prospect of the mission he and Hestia were about to embark upon, and he wondered if his accomplice felt the same nervous excitement.

Ezekiel knew all that he risked by assisting Hestia in uncovering dark family secrets—his father's employment, his family's well being, and his own future. All would be in great jeopardy the moment he stepped beyond the threshold of his quarters. However, he could not deny the heavy beating in his chest when Hestia smiled upon him. He could not forget the excited gleam in her eyes when she explained her plan and how contagious her spontaneity was. Logic recited every reason why this mission was unwise. But his heart spoke louder, and it told him to take this chance.

"Son, come get something to eat before we head out," Ambrose called from the kitchen nook.

Ezekiel snapped from his reverie and darted one last longing look at Deston Manor before rising from his bed.

Hestia lay awake in her chamber. The sun barely shone through the clouds, yet her mind was buzzing with activity. Her eyes gazed at the ceiling as she played through the steps of her plan. She knew her plan must be executed flawlessly, for it was not only her safety at risk now. She was surprised that Ezekiel had agreed to join her so readily. After years of having her inquisitiveness met with swift rebuffs, she appreciated that someone was finally willing to show her support.

Hestia breathed deeply through her nose in an attempt to slow the pounding in her chest. Jessamine would be in to fetch her soon. It would be crucial that she be none the wiser to the day's hidden schedule. The handmaiden was as eagle-eyed as they came and would surely catch on to any small change in her everyday countenance. She proved this just yesterday when she questioned her on the simple act of being more quiet than usual. Still, her breath occasionally hitched at the thought of the day's impending events.

A light rapping at the door brought Hestia back to reality as Jessamine tiptoed in. "Dearie, it's time to—oh, you're awake," Jessamine said with a start. "How long have you been up?"

"Um, not long," Hestia said, silently chastising herself for not pretending to be asleep when Jessamine walked in.

"You didn't have another one of those nightmares, did you?" Jessamine's brows furrowed.

"Oh, no. Perhaps my body is just anticipating the excitement of yet another wonderful day at Deston."

The sarcastic comment earned Hestia a sideways glance from her handmaiden before she walked over and pulled the covers off of her. "Up and at 'em!" Jessamine got Hestia out of bed and helped her prepare for the day ahead.

As Hestia washed, Jessamine prattled on about the young girl's schedule. "You have your lessons with Ms. Evans at eight, and then lunch at noon, as usual . . ."

As Jessamine continued, Hestia braced herself for facing Priscilla. While Hestia had grown rather adept at putting Jessamine off any potential mischief, Priscilla was an altogether different beast. Though they had been acquainted for only a couple of days, the governess' eyes saw more than Hestia herself could imagine. She would have to steel herself to a far greater degree to betray those piercing orbs.

"Hestia, do I still have your attention?"

Priscilla's question snapped Hestia out of her daydream. "Oh, yes, yes, Ms. Evans. My apologies." She flashed Priscilla a false smile. "I did not sleep very well last night, so please forgive me if my attention is rather lacking this morning."

Priscilla eyed Hestia in concern. "Well, that is quite alright, Hestia. Why don't we change to a more appealing subject. Literature." Priscilla pulled a couple of books from her side and handed one to Hestia. "I know that tradition dictates that literature be reserved for males, but I personally see nothing wrong with bending tradition a bit, especially as your handmaiden has told me that you possess a particular proclivity for certain novels."

That must have been what they discussed the other day, Hestia thought. "Jessamine feels that I should be reading 'gentler things,'" Hestia noted. "Music sheets and sewing guides."

"Yes, she mentioned that to me as well. So, perhaps we just keep this lesson between ourselves." Priscilla winked, and Hestia smiled, feeling, for the first time, almost comfortable in her governess' presence. A sigh then escaped Priscilla's lips. "Hestia, I know that there may still be some questions regarding my . . . behavior since I have arrived here."

Hestia thought back to the odd look Priscilla gave her when they first met, the sleepwalking episode, and the few cryptic words they had exchanged since.

"But I assure you that everything will be made clear in time. In the interim, however, I . . . want to ensure that you trust me. It is a complicated process. I promise that my primary goal is to serve your best interest. I just need your confidence and patience."

"Ms. Evans, I appreciate that you value honesty so strongly. And I understand that you believe that time is required so I may better understand the truth you want to tell. But *I* can assure *you* that I am capable of handling more than you may think. Which is why I must know . . ." Hestia trailed off for a moment as she looked into Priscilla's inquiring eyes. She scooted closer and placed both hands on Priscilla's. "Ms. Evans, how did you know my mother?"

The air in the drawing room hung thick with the weight of Hestia's question.

Priscilla's face took on a look of dread. She released Hestia's hand and stood up. She opened her mouth as if to speak, but gave no more than a tired sigh. She then turned away from Hestia and walked toward the window.

Silence pervaded the room for many moments before at last, it was broken.

"That night, when you found me in the hallway, that was the first bout of night walking I had experienced in many years. As a young girl, I spent most of my time indulging in fantastical stories. These stories filled me with such night terrors that I often sleep-walked through the halls of my family's estate, crying and shouting. My parents finally took to locking the doors to my chamber at night to keep me from frightening my older sister. As I grew, I assumed I had finally outgrown them. I never imagined they'd return so abruptly."

Hestia's dream came to mind; the blood, the blue door, and the figures whose faces she could never quite make out. "I've had the same horrible dream for months now. And every time, more details reveal themselves. It terrifies me, especially since certain parts of it feel so . . . familiar," Hestia said.

"What about it feels so familiar to you?"

"There's this blue door that I swear I have seen before, but I cannot seem to recall where. And there's a woman. I can never fully see her face, but somehow, it feels as if she is . . . someone I know."

Priscilla suddenly rushed toward Hestia and grabbed her hands. "This woman, is there anything you can make out about her? Any striking features?" Priscilla's grip around her wrists tightened, making Hestia wince.

"Ms. Evans," Hestia began, but Priscilla continued to strengthen her grip. "Ms. Evans, I—"

"What on earth is going on here?"

Both women jumped at the voice, and Priscilla dropped Hestia's wrists. Jessamine stood at the drawing room's threshold, eyes wide.

"I think we should cut our lesson short today, Lady Rosewood." Priscilla gathered her books, parchments, and quills. "If you'll excuse me, I must . . . must go lay down." Priscilla swiftly exited the drawing room, leaving Hestia's mind swirling with unanswered questions.

"Dearie, are you alright?" Jessamine hurried to Hestia's side. "I was just walking by and saw Ms. Evans' hands on you."

"I am fine, Jessamine." Hestia heard the lie leave her lips. "Ms. Evans didn't mean anything by it. I think she was just tired and acting out of sorts."

Jessamine eyed Hestia out of concern before gathering Hestia's items. "There is still about an hour or so until lunch."

"I will practice my sewing until then."

"Very good, dearie," Jessamine said. She turned to leave, but paused for a moment, her mouth opening, as if a question perched just on the end of her tongue. But she closed it again and made her way out of the room.

Hestia was left alone, a million thoughts, concerns, and curiosities spinning through her young mind. *Ms. Priscilla Evans, who exactly* are *you?*

After the hour that felt like a day finally ticked away, Jessamine returned to fetch Hestia for lunch.

"Have you heard from Ms. Evans?" Hestia innocently inquired.

"No, ma'am," Jessamine replied. "I reckon she may still be resting."

A mixture of concern and elation flooded Hestia's heart, though she endeavored to keep her manner even in front of her handmaiden. "Well, I do hope that some extra sleep will put her in a better state."

Jessamine led Hestia out of the drawing room toward the dining area for lunch. As Hestia's earlier interaction with Priscilla had failed to answer her primary question, she knew that it was now time to put her previous plan into action. As the pair walked down the hall, Hestia peered out the same window as she had the day before. However, on this day she found, to her dismay, a gray, dreary sky. *How am I to convince Jessamine that I wish to dine outside in this weather?* "Jessamine," Hestia began, stopping the handmaiden. "I would very much like to dine outside again for lunch today."

Jessamine looked out the window. "Are you sure, dearie? It is quite gray out today."

"It is, but . . . but I have heard much about the benefits of daily fresh air, especially for a woman as young and delicate as I." Jessamine raised an eyebrow, but Hestia continued to plead. "Please, Jessamine. Uncle rarely allows me to step outside the manor when he is home." Hestia batted her eyelashes as the handmaiden took one last look at her.

Finally, she let out a long sigh and relented. "I will go talk to Hiram and get everything set up. I have to do some extra work around the manor this afternoon anyhow."

"Oh, thank you Jessamine!" Hestia said, wrapping her arms around the woman.

No more than ten minutes later, Hestia was alone, quickly swallowing her plate of fish and slurping her tea in a most unladylike manner to finish in enough time to meet Ezekiel. As the birds and insects flitted about the garden, her eyes scanned the expanse of trees, shrubs, and other plant life. She felt the minutes fall away, yet did not yet see any sign of the gardener's boy. *Where is he?*

She worried he may have gotten cold feet, that the prospect of getting caught proved too much for him to bear. She knew that each moment that passed drew her further from the secrets she so desperately needed to uncover, especially given that they only had one hour with which to work.

Just when Hestia finished the last bite of her lunch, she caught movement out of the corner of her eye. She turned and saw a long arm wave in her direction. Ezekiel's face held a crooked smile, his eyes bright, though somewhat hidden beneath his blond mop of hair. Hestia smiled back and motioned for him to come closer. As the boy gingerly walked toward her, Hestia took note of his walk, so unsure and yet, so comfortable. But as quickly as she felt her heart putter in her chest, she pushed the sensation away, returning her focus to the task at hand.

As Ezekiel drew closer, Hestia stood up to greet him. "I thought you'd had a change of heart."

"Oh, no," Ezekiel said. "My father, he's been eating slower these days. I always help him clean up and prepare for his afternoon rest before I come outside. He just took an especially long time today."

"That's sweet of you to care for him so."

"He's all I've got."

A pang hit Hestia's heart as she was reminded of what she was asking Ezekiel to risk for her. Taking a deep breath, she said, "Are you ready to uncover some secrets, my friend? I had another interaction with Ms. Evans this morning that confirmed something is hiding beneath the surface." Hestia gave Ezekiel a brief synopsis of her lesson with Priscilla, including her strange reaction to hearing Hestia's dream.

"It *does* sound like she is hiding something," Ezekiel agreed.

"Which is why it is more important now than ever that we discover what that something is."

"Are you sure that you don't want to just wait until Ms. Evans feels comfortable enough to tell you herself?"

"I have spent all of my life wanting to know more about my parents, only to be met with odd looks, half-truths, and anger. Now, I finally have an opportunity to learn something real. And to know that this opportunity sits under my own roof, I simply cannot abide by anyone's schedule but my own. I will force it if I have to, but the truth *will* be revealed."

Ezekiel looked into Hestia's eyes, burning with desire and determination. He felt his cheeks flush slightly and looked away. "What items am I to look for in Ms. Evans' quarters?"

"Documents, photographs, anything that may mention my mother, Helena," Hestia replied.

"And where will you be?"

"I will be just outside the door, keeping watch to ensure no one catches us."

"The other servants won't come by there?"

"Hiram keeps to the kitchen, and Jessamine and Adella will not usually disrupt an area where someone is asleep. We should be safe, as long as we move quickly and return to our posts before the hour is up."

"We should probably move then," Ezekiel said. "We don't have much time left."

"Yes, follow me." Hestia waved her hand, and the two sleuths swiftly made their way toward the manor's entrance.

Once they arrived at the entrance, Ezekiel nervously looked up. Hestia placed her hand in his and gave it a generous squeeze. Ezekiel turned his gaze to her with that same crooked smile, and together, the two pushed the manor's doors open, welcoming the perilous journey ahead.

Once Hestia and Ezekiel slipped inside, they allowed themselves a moment to adjust their eyes to the dim interior. The large foyer in which they stood introduced the musty odor that pervaded the whole of the manor. The wooden floors had the characteristic shine of being freshly washed. "Jessamine and Adella have already been through here," Hestia whispered, pointing to the floor. "So, we should be safe for now." She leaned down to remove her shoes, using Ezekiel's shoulder for support.

Ezekiel was grateful that there wasn't more light to reveal his surely reddening face as Hestia's hand lay upon him. Once she finished removing her shoes, Ezekiel followed suit, and the pair, footwear in hand, tiptoed toward the first hallway.

As he walked behind Hestia, the young gardener took in the sights that he had not had an opportunity to fully view upon his first visit inside the manor. He noted the stately architecture, high ceilings, and delicate artwork that lined the walls. While he appreciated Hestia's plight, he *did* wonder at that moment why she would voluntarily court trouble when such luxury lay at her fingertips. Ezekiel imagined the parties they would throw, the meals they would enjoy, only if his father was lord of the manor. He had never known the noble life. And yet, somehow, the act of being inside of a manor seemed wholly comfortable.

"We are here," Hestia said, breaking Ezekiel from his reverie.

He shook his head, finding himself in front of a much smaller, but still quite stately, door.

"Just beyond this door is Ms. Evans' sleeping quarters. Beyond here, lies the truth."

"Well," Ezekiel began. "It is now or never, I suppose."

The gardener boy looked at Hestia, who gave him an appreciative and reassuring smile. She motioned for him to hand her his footwear, which he obliged. "I will be right here. If I cough twice, that means someone is coming."

"Right," Ezekiel replied.

"Good luck, my friend. And thank you. I cannot begin to tell you what this means to me." Hestia beamed brightly at Ezekiel.

Ezekiel nodded and slowly reached his hand out, turning the knob to Priscilla's quarters.

CHAPTER SIX

Ezekiel said a silent prayer as the door to Priscilla's quarters opened before him. He moved forward, slipping through before quietly closing the door behind him.

The small bit of light emanating from the room's window helped him make out the scene before him. The room was small and plain; only a four-poster bed and a simple night table stood against the far wall. He breathed deeply through his nose when he saw Priscilla Evans curled upon the bed, sound asleep. As he continued to scan the room, he came upon what appeared to be a small brown suitcase nestled in the corner. *That must be the one Hestia was talking about,* Ezekiel thought. He crept closer, each step making his heart race and palms sweat. Mere inches from the suitcase, he found it empty.

Knowing his time was limited, he frantically looked about until his eyes landed on the night table. Only a foot or so from Priscilla's face, it held all manner of books and parchments, some of which, Ezekiel hoped, would hold the answers Hestia sought. He snuck across the floor, stopping only once as a board creaked beneath. Ezekiel froze as Priscilla turned over and remained utterly motionless until he heard her breathing return to its resting rhythm. With a small sigh of relief, he continued tiptoeing toward the nightstand.

Once he reached his destination, he made quick work of scanning the papers and books on top. He saw notes, translations, and other items pertaining to her role as governess. As he searched, his eyes occasionally flitted toward Priscilla to check that she remained asleep. The woman lay on her side in the fetal position, her sunken features illuminated by the sun's dim rays and her eyes appearing to twitch, as if in a dream. Ezekiel reached a shaking hand out to move one of the books on the stand next.

"No . . ."

The word was uttered so quietly that Ezekiel was scarcely sure he heard it at first. He pulled his hand away just as the sound repeated.

"No . . ."

Ezekiel watched as Priscilla's brow furrowed, seeming to be angry or in agony. Unconsciously, he held his breath.

"Helena."

Suddenly, as if the name had been a spell, Priscilla's face fell, and she returned to a state of natural sleep.

Hestia's mother.

Spurred on to not waste another moment, Ezekiel moved the book, a piece of parchment falling out of its pages and floating to the floor in front of him. It was torn on one side, as if ripped from a larger book. Ezekiel picked it up to examine it further and recognized it to be a workhouse record. *Why would she have this?* He traced his finger down the long list of names until he came upon Priscilla's own. As he scanned the notes near her name, one particular note made his blood suddenly run cold.

Quickly and carefully, he folded the parchment and shoved it into the pocket of his trousers. As he motioned to return the book to its perch, he noticed another item fall from its pages. Leaning down, Ezekiel picked it up and discovered that it was an old photograph of two young girls. One girl faced away from the camera and the other beamed brightly at the lens. On instinct, he turned the photograph over and noticed writing on the back:

Helena and Fidelia Ward, June 29th, 1827

Of course, she looks just like Hestia. Ezekiel shoved the photograph in his pocket with the parchment and placed the book back on the nightstand. *This'll be enough, I'm sure,* Ezekiel thought. Satisfied with his finds, the young boy backed away from the nightstand and made his way quietly back to the door. Just as Ezekiel reached out and grabbed the knob, he heard two very small, but clear, coughs. *Brilliant.*

He pulled his hand away and waited, hoping that whoever intruded would depart swiftly.

———— ✦ ————

Hestia watched and waited outside Priscilla's door. Her mind filled with musings as to the activities that were taking place on the other side. The very prospect of learning more about her family brought Hestia a comfort that she had rarely felt in her life. While she knew that she could not change the past, knowing more about where she came from would free her from the chains of uncertainty that seemed to increase as each year passed in Deston Manor.

If Ms. Evans knew my mother, then maybe she knows how she died. The thought made Hestia's stomach drop. It was a burning question, one most integral to her own internal healing. However, her mind could not help but loop back to the instances in which she questioned August about the fate of her parents, only to be met with ignorance, and finally, pure rage. Something about her uncle's reaction always stayed with her, adding to the unease she felt toward him. If the information discovered today altered her feelings further, would she be able to keep silent upon his return?

All of these thoughts and emotions stirred wildly within the young woman as she waited for Ezekiel. She watched the door before her carefully—so carefully that she barely noticed a figure appear next to her until she caught it in her periphery. "Adella!" Hestia startled as the housemaid stood next to her.

Adella nodded at Hestia and moved her eyes down to the two pairs of shoes the girl held in her hands.

Drat, Hestia thought. *How will I ever explain this?* She coughed twice. "I was just . . . having my lunch, when I noticed a stain on the bottom of my shoe. I came in and took them off to give to Jessamine, but then I noticed this other pair in the foyer. I thought they may belong to Ms. Evans, but it seems she is still asleep, so I will have to come back to question her." The words left Hestia's mouth so clumsily she doubted the housemaid believed a word of it.

Even so, Adella smiled at the young woman and reached for her hand. She placed a small piece of parchment inside of it before turning and leaving the hallway.

Hestia waited until the housemaid disappeared around the corner before reading it:

I'd suggest you both move quickly. Good luck!

Hestia's eye snapped toward the space the housemaid once occupied. *How did she—?* The thought refused to fully form as Hestia shook her head and leaned against the door in front of her. "The coast is clear. Quickly!" She whispered.

A few seconds later, Priscilla's door opened, and the young man slipped out, shutting it behind him.

Hestia immediately noticed a change in his countenance. His face was extremely pale, and his brow was furrowed. His gray eyes locked onto Hestia's own and refused to let go, as if doing so would mean an end to his life. *He found something.* A sudden chill ran up her spine as she looked at the poor gardener's boy. She took a deep breath. "What did you find?"

Ezekiel looked at Hestia for another moment before pro-
ducing two items from his pocket. He hesitantly pushed them in
Hestia's direction.

She dropped the shoes at her feet and took the items from
Ezekiel's hand, first examining the photograph of the two girls.
The young brunette appeared unfamiliar, and much of her face
was obscured by the angle. However, the blonde's features, even
at such a young age, were utterly unmistakable. "My mother,"
Hestia whispered.

"Turn it over."

Hestia followed and saw the inscription across the back.
"Helena and Fidelia Ward?" She flipped the photo back around
and studied it carefully. "Who is Fidelia Ward?"

"I don't know," Ezekiel said. "From that photograph, I'm
guessing they may have been sisters."

"I . . . I have an aunt." Hestia stared at the photograph for
some time, allowing the faces of the young girls to burn into her
memory. The young brunette, her aunt, may still be alive. Hestia's
heart leapt at this prospect. "Why would Ms. Evans have this?"

"I don't know," Ezekiel replied. "But Ms. Evans' story
gets odder. Look at the other parchment I gave you." As Hestia
began to open the document, Ezekial said, "It's from an old workhouse record."

Hestia scanned the names, dates, and notes scrawled
across the page. She finally approached Ms. Evans' name and followed her finger across the information listed, reading aloud what
she saw. "Priscilla Evans," Hestia began. "Date of birth, April 19,
1819. Date of—" She looked up at Ezekiel, eyes wide, before continuing. "Date of expiration, May 18, 1850. Cause: Scarlet Fever."
Hestia's breathing grew erratic, and she felt the room around her
begin to spin. She looked at the door, whose room contained a
supposed corpse in perfect repose. "Why—" Hestia began, but
fear and confusion closed her throat.

Just as Ezekiel opened his mouth to respond, the manor
clocks announced the hour.

"We have to go," Hestia said, still holding onto the findings.

They quickly scooped up their footwear and made for the manor doors. Once they threw their shoes back on and exited the manor, Hestia wrapped her arms around Ezekiel's shoulders and pulled him in tightly.

"Thank you, Ezekiel. You have no idea how thankful I am for your help."

Ezekiel felt his ears burn. "Just . . . stay safe, Hestia," he squeaked out.

With that, the pair unraveled and ran toward their required destinations. Once Hestia reached her lunch table, she hurriedly folded Priscilla's photograph and parchment and slipped them into the book she had placed on the table. Right as she sat down, Jessamine approached from the back.

"All set, dearie?" Jessamine asked.

"Oh, yes, Jessamine," Hestia replied. "Please tell Hiram that this was a most delicious meal."

Jessamine gathered her dishes and Hestia grabbed her book. As the two women walked back inside the manor, the excitement of the afternoon caught up with Hestia and made the poor girl sway in place.

"Dearie, are you alright?"

"I think I may need to lie down for a bit, Jessamine. Perhaps I got a little too much fresh air today." The ease with which each subsequent lie was falling from Hestia's lips made her even more lightheaded. She hated having to keep secrets from her handmaiden, but knew it was for the good of everyone.

As Jessamine settled Hestia in her bedchamber for an afternoon slumber, another occupant of Deston Manor began to stir. Within a moment's time, this woman would rise from her bed, light her lamp, and notice that the papers on her nightstand were not in the exact position in which she left them. Upon further inspection, she would discover the disappearance of two very important items. She would tear apart what little was in the room before accepting the truth—the pieces were gone.

Soon, Ms. Evans would be forced to confront the fate that she knew would eventually come for her.

CHAPTER SEVEN

That night, as Hestia turned in her bed, that familiar dream began its ritualistic dance through her mind.

A white gown, a tall male figure. They smile, their faces blank. Blond locks sway as the male's hands grip the gown, balling it tightly beneath clenched fists. When he lets go, a crimson stain stamps the gown as the woman falls limp in his arms. The handprint stain spreads until the entire dress is blood red. A male voice whispers, "'Til death do us part." The scene pulls back rapidly, and a pale-blue door slams, bloody fingerprints coating the doorknob.

Hestia awoke with a start, her heart beating rapidly. As she pulled herself up and looked around, the shadows of her bedchamber informed her that it was still nightfall. *Why does that door seem so familiar?* This was now the third time it had appeared in her dream, locking the figures away, as if locking away a horrible secret. However, Hestia did not have much time to ponder before she heard a soft yet urgent rapping on her chamber door. Slowly, she rose from her bed and approached the door. "Who is it?" She whispered.

"Hestia, I must speak with you immediately."

All of the hair on Hestia's arms stood on end as she recognized the unmistakable whisper of Priscilla Evans. Her eyes darted to her nightstand, whereupon nestled the book that contained Priscilla's stolen photo and parchment.

"One moment!" Hestia deftly raced over and slipped the book under her pillow before returning to her chamber door. Despite the fear that coursed through every vein, she steeled herself and cracked it open.

Without a moment's pause, Priscilla shoved the door all the way open and invited herself inside, closing the door gingerly behind her.

Even in the dark, Hestia could sense the panic in Priscilla's expression. Forcing aside her unease, she decided to feign innocence until the governess made the first move. "Ms. Evans," Hestia began, rubbing her eyes. "To what do I owe such a late-night visit?"

"Sit," Priscilla said.

Too tired to argue, she obliged.

"Hestia, I know that you are, by nature, a curious girl. Your mother was very much the same. You deserve to know everything there is to know about your family, but that does not give you the right to steal from your governess."

Hestia continued to play dumb. "Ms. Evans, whatever are you on about?"

Priscilla stepped closer to Hestia, her piercing eyes fixed on her.

Hestia began to squirm uneasily, her eyes almost imperceptibly glancing to her bed.

Catching the movement, Priscilla made a mad dash toward the girl's bed and tore the pillows off, revealing the book beneath. Priscilla opened the book to a random page and gave it a good shake. Sure enough, two worn pieces of paper fluttered down to the floor. Priscilla picked up the photograph and parchment in triumph and turned back to Hestia. "Oh, Hestia, I did not want to believe that you would stoop so low as to commit thievery. But when I realized that these two items were missing from my possessions, something told me that I would find them with you."

As the initial shock began to fade and the reality of Hestia's situation sunk in, she felt her face flush with anger and a hint of cockiness. Dropping all pretense of innocence, she stood, hands upon her hips, and flashed her governess a stone-faced expression. "Yes, Ms. Evans, I have your items. All my life, I have either been denied the truth or told to wait for a day that never comes to learn the truth. So, I took matters into my own hands." Hestia snatched the documents back from Priscilla, holding up the photograph in her left hand first. "The blonde girl is my mother. There is no mistaking our resemblance. Plus, her name is written on the back. I don't know why you have this, but I do know that this provides further proof that you knew my mother. And this—" Hestia put her left hand down and picked up her right, which held the workhouse record. "This is simply beyond all explanation."

All resolve melted away from Priscilla's face, replaced by a look of defeat.

"According to this parchment, Ms. Priscilla Evans is dead. Now, either I have been taking lessons from a spectre, or—" Hestia felt herself beginning to spiral, so she took a breath and leaned closer to Priscilla until their faces were mere inches apart. "Ms. Evans, who exactly *are* you?"

The question hung in the air of Hestia's bedchamber like a thick fog as Priscilla and Hestia stared each other down. Finally, Priscilla let out a deep sigh and closed her eyes.

Hestia watched in confusion as a single tear rolled down her cheek.

"You *are* so much like your mother," Priscilla whispered, looking back up at Hestia's face. "And for that, I am truly grateful. I will tell you all that you wish to know. But I must warn you, Hestia, what you learn from the story I am about to tell may vastly alter the life you have grown accustomed to." Priscilla reached a hand out to Hestia and gestured for the photograph. When Hestia handed it to her, she held it up so they could both see it. "This photograph is one of my most prized possessions. It was taken during a much simpler, happier time. A time when your mother was free and when she and I were nearly inseparable."

Hestia inched closer and examined the brunette girl in the photograph more carefully. She could not make out much of her features, but as she glanced from the profile in the photo to the profile of the woman who stood before her, realization suddenly began to dawn. "Ms. Evans?"

With a soft smile, the governess pointed to the brunette in the photograph. "This young woman is named Fidelia Ward. She is the younger sister of your mother, Helena. And, she is also the woman who stands before you tonight."

CHAPTER EIGHT

Hestia plopped herself upon her bed as the gravity of Fidelia's confession overcame her.

"Perhaps we *should* sit," Fidelia said, joining her.

"So, you . . ." Hestia began. "You are my—"

"Aunt, yes."

Hestia sighed as the words settled into her mind. She looked at the woman she formerly knew to be Ms. Priscilla Evans, now her own blood relation. "Where have you been all this time?" Hestia suddenly snapped. She regretted it immediately as she saw Fidelia wince.

"Trust me, Hestia, I would have come sooner if I could have. But certain events had to align to ensure my mission would be facilitated correctly."

"Mission? You say that as if you have intended to come save me."

"I *have* come to save you."

A chill ran down Hestia's spine, accompanied by a look of great concern.

"Let's start at the beginning." Fidelia shifted on the bed and settled in to tell her tale. "Your mother and I led exceedingly simple lives growing up. Any nobility you currently possess comes solely from your father's blood. Our father, your maternal grandfather, was a coal miner, and our mother, your grandmother, worked at the schoolhouse until she became pregnant with your mother. Once Helena was born, our mother devoted herself to homemaking and caring for her children. We were far from possessing any material wealth, but we got by just as well as any family could. We lived in a small cottage just outside of Deston."

A smile flitted across Fidelia's face as she recalled a particularly happy moment from her childhood. "On cold winter nights, your mother and I would sit in front of our fireplace, making shadow puppets on the walls. And once our parents began to doze, we would take turns at scaring each other with fantastical stories of ghosts, dragons, and all manner of vicious beasts. I was always the first to be spooked, of course. But I would get Helena back, as her stories would fill me with such terrible nightmares that I would begin to sleepwalk and give her a good fright. Why, after my first sleepwalking episode, your mother was so distraught that she did not speak to me that entire following morning. She had thought that the bogeyman had come to steal her away!"

Both Fidelia and Hestia chuckled as Hestia imagined her aunt and mother as precocious young girls.

"Your mother, despite what came bumping in the night, was always so much braver than she ever gave herself credit for. Certainly, much braver than *I* ever was. I dare say if the bogeyman *had* come for her in those days, she would have sent him running with his tail between his legs. She was my fiercest protector from the world's true evils." Fidelia looked at her niece and brushed a thin hand across her face. "You remind me so much of her. Your tenacity, your beauty. She would be proud of the young woman you have become."

"Uncle always says that he sees much of my mother in me. I just wish I would have known her as well as you both had." She noticed Fidelia's hand flinch away from her face at the mention of August. Quickly, she decided to change the subject, lest her aunt decide to cut her story short. "Were you there when my mother first met my father . . . Aunt Fidelia?"

Fidelia beamed as she heard herself addressed by her niece. "If you wish, you may call me Aunt Delia. Delia is what your mother always called me."

"Alright," Hestia replied. "Did you know my father, Aunt Delia?"

"Yes, I was there for their first meeting. Growing up, your mother was always the beauty of the two of us. While I inherited many of our father's strong features, Helena was blessed with the softer, more agreeable features befitting a true lady. Shiny golden locks, bright green eyes. It was no wonder many men lined our cottage in an attempt to court her. Your mother was not only beautiful, however. She also possessed a sharp wit and an incredible emotional depth. So, she would not be satisfied with any simple man. One evening, not long before we met your father, my mother had just turned away yet another unfortunate suitor for Helena. Work in the mines was slowing, and money was growing scarce, so she begged her to choose a mate that would save us from the poorhouse. Your mother looked her straight in the eye and said, 'Mother, the other half of my heart lies out there somewhere, and I refuse to settle until I find it.' Oh, her stubbornness brought our parents such grief. But she did not give in. And then one day . . ." Fidelia trailed off as the memory began to get the better of her.

"A few days later, Helena and I were heading into town with the little money we had left to barter for food. As we walked along the horse-path, a grand carriage approached from behind. Your mother and I moved to allow it to pass, but the driver was so tired, he hardly recognized how close his horses came to the edge until they about ran us over. I, clumsy as I was, fell into a large mud pile and received a great bruise on my right hip. Your mother shouted at the carriage driver, which summoned the two occupants of the carriage to pop their heads out of the window. Seeing Helena, they commanded that the driver halt the carriage."

"Was one of the occupants my father?" Hestia inquired, to which Fidelia gave an affirmative nod.

"While some of the men who had attempted to court your mother were certainly wealthy, we had never before come face to face with the noble class. But Jonathan Rosewood made quick work of winning your mother over, first by making amends for nearly running her and her sister off the road. He actually approached us from the carriage, took *my* hand first, and kissed it in apology. Once I knew him better, I teased him for that act, as he ended up with a bit of mud on his lips." Fidelia laughed. "But when he took your mother's hand next, it was as if something shifted in the air. I could tell by the look in both of their eyes that their meeting was fated."

"You said there were two occupants in the carriage. Was the other one my uncle?" While Hestia adored hearing stories of her parents, she also wondered what August must have been like in his younger years.

As if being snapped out of a trance, Fidelia's face darkened, and she nodded. "Yes, it was your uncle."

"What was he like back then?"

"He . . . was very much as I assume he is now. He stood close to the carriage, but even from where I stood, I could make out his features. His hair was darker than it is now, but he had the same pale face and stoic personality. When he finally came over to us and Jonathan introduced him as his brother, I was quite shocked. They seemed in every way to be like night and day."

"If Uncle had met you before, how was this not brought up when he hired you as my governess?" Hestia questioned.

"Well, I suppose I was so covered in mud that my features were scarcely visible. That first meeting with your uncle was the only time I ever *truly* interacted with him, until our recent arrangement, of course. He did not attend your parents' wedding, and our lives were fairly separate, with him keeping to the manor anytime Jonathan and Helena came to visit us. Besides, the second he attempted to express his displeasure at being delayed by our presence that day, your mother chided him severely, and suddenly, I was all but a memory. I'll never forget the look he gave your mother as she spoke back to him. I don't think he had ever had a woman speak to him in such a way. He seemed shocked and oddly . . . enamored."

Hestia picked up on her discomfort and gave her aunt's hand a small squeeze.

"I suppose it wasn't too unusual, as many men reacted that way upon seeing your mother," Fidelia said, shaking her head. "I just wish I would have seen it for what it truly was at the time . . . At any rate, your mother was absolutely smitten with the noble Jonathan Rosewood from that day forward. I had begun to think I'd never see your mother fall for any man, so to see her fall as hard and fast as she did for your father, I knew he was special. And little did we know that he was just as caught in her web as she was in his. Your father visited our cottage only a few days after our excursion to express his interest in courting your mother. I remember the look on my mother's face when she opened the door to your father. She was so overcome with excitement, she nearly leaned down and kissed his feet! I still think my parents only saw your father as evidence that Helena had finally come around to marrying someone wealthy, a means to escape the poorhouse, but I knew better. There was no denying the look in their eyes when they were with each other. Your parents were soulmates."

Hestia stared at Fidelia as she imagined her parents both so deeply in love.

"Only a few months passed before their courtship developed further, and your father announced his intent to marry my sister. She was only seventeen at the time, but she was so eager to accept the responsibilities of a lord's wife. In the days leading up to the wedding, we hardly saw her. We lived only a short ten-minute carriage ride from the manor, but she spent nearly every hour of every day here, training and becoming familiar with noble living. In those rare moments when I *did* see her, I dare say I never saw her look so radiantly happy." Fidelia stopped as a cry stuck in her throat.

"What was their wedding like?" Hestia inquired, intent to distract her aunt's grief.

Choking back a small sob, Fidelia took a deep breath and continued. "It was truly spectacular, just as we imagined their life together would be. Your grandfather, Thaddeus Rosewood, who still served as lord of the manor at that time, had taken quite fondly to your mother. He spared no expense to ensure that they had nothing but the best for their nuptials. Shortly after the wedding, your mother moved here to Deston Manor. The day she left for good, our little cottage felt so dark, so cold. It was as if she had taken all of the sunshine with her."

"Did she at least visit?"

"Oh, yes, as much as she could, given her new duties. And she would write. She even wanted us to live at the manor with her, and had actually convinced Thaddeus to offer my parents and I lodging. But my parents, as unwaveringly proud as they were, refused. So, I stayed behind as well to care for them. They *did* accept stipends and food from the manor, however, upon Helena's insistence. Your mother went to great lengths to ensure we were never forgotten."

"When my mother would visit you, after she began living here, was she still the same?"

"In the beginning, yes. She would regale me with tales of her new life but always with that same wit, humor, and warmth that was uniquely hers. She was absolutely suited to her new duties and found beauty in every crack and crevice of this manor. And her love for your father overflowed with each syllable. However, after a few months, I began to sense that, just underneath that cheery disposition, something was nagging at her. Something that she did not quite want to share with me just yet. Being the agreeable sister I was, I didn't pry at the time. Thinking back on it now, I should have. But, as it was, I would not have had time to pry. For by the time my suspicions truly arose, your mother announced that she was pregnant with you."

"So, you still spoke to my mother when she was pregnant with me?"

"Oh, more than that. I actually held you when you were only days old. Your mother came to visit us, and I instantly fell in love with you. Even as a baby, you looked so much like your mother." Fidelia reached out and brushed a lock of Hestia's blonde hair behind her ear. "How I wish the rest of your life could have been as blissful as those first two years."

"Two years? Why only two years?" Hestia questioned.

"Your mother would bring you to visit our parents and I at least once a week," Fidelia replied. "On special occasions, your father would even join her. Seeing you was a bright spot in my life for so long. But unfortunately, that all changed soon after your second birthday." Fidelia's face fell once more.

Hestia shifted as she anticipated what was to come next.

"I do not presume to know the etiquette of the nobility, Hestia. All that I know at this point was told to me by your mother when she wrote to me. Apparently, it had been assumed that, upon the eventual demise of the Rosewood patriarch, all assets and responsibilities would be inherited by the eldest son, your uncle August. However, one day, Thaddeus sat your mother, father, and uncle down to announce that all aspects of his legacy were to be passed down to Jonathan."

"So, Uncle would never receive any inheritance?"

"No. And, once this news was shared, both your mother and father had expected to be on the receiving end of one of your uncle's greatest rages. Helena had already told me a bit about August's short temper and expected the worst."

Hestia thought back to the fit he had directed at her when she had inquired into her parents' deaths. She now assumed the depth of that rage had barely scratched the surface of its capability.

"However, what she experienced instead confused her and, though I knew she wouldn't admit it, shook her to her very core. After hearing that he would not receive the inheritance or title of lord of the manor after all, August locked himself away and did not rejoin the family for three days. The only signs of life were from the servants, who brought him collections of books, the topics of which your mother could never quite make out. When he finally reappeared, he was, as your mother put it, uncharac-teristically calm. As if whatever he had done while in his study had brought him a sense of peace. She said that he congratulated your father on his impending inheritance and continued on as if nothing had happened."

"Aunt Delia, when we first met, you surmised that my uncle makes me uncomfortable. Do you remember that interaction?"

"I do."

"That was not an . . . incorrect assumption."

"I didn't think it was."

"I used to implore Uncle repeatedly to tell me more about the fates that befell my parents. At first, he provided me with vague formalities, until a few months ago, when he must have felt that I had pushed too far."

"He unleashed his rage on you?" Fidelia guessed.

Hestia nodded.

"Did he hit you or harm you in any way?"

"No, but he sent me to bed without supper. Ever since that day, my interactions with him have been largely formal and uneasy. Jessamine tries to encourage me to open up to him, but something tells me I shouldn't."

"Your handmaiden means well, Hestia, but I doubt that *she* even knows the truth of who your uncle is."

"Do you think—" Hestia paused, her hands shaking as her next words formed a lump in her throat. She let out a sharp exhale before continuing. "Do you think that Uncle had something to do with the deaths of my mother and father?"

"I will first admit to you that I have never had any concrete evidence upon which to support my suspicions. Your mother's words, coupled with my own intuition, are all that I have ever relied on. Helena spoke very little of your uncle when she met with or wrote to me, but she did tell me of his rages and his habit of leering at her as she read in the drawing room or took tea in the kitchen. She would try to brush it off, and no matter how many times I encouraged her to do so, she never told your father nor your grandfather about the unease she felt. She would just say that she could not bring herself to slander a member of the family. Her love for Jonathan and Thaddeus far out-weighed her instincts at that time, I'm afraid. But after those three days, August's countenance completely changed and his advances on your mother became much more obvious. During one supper, he actually took Helena's hand in his own, much to your mother's shock."

"What did my father do? Or my grandfather?"

"Unfortunately, neither were at supper that night. They both had a great deal on their plates, especially as Thaddeus was getting on in years and needed to ensure that your father had all he needed to take things over. But when Helena was able to tell Jonathan about the events at supper, he promised her that he would discuss it with August during a trip they were about to take. Little did any of us know what would transpire. It was nearly one week after your father, grandfather, and uncle left that your mother brought you to the cottage for a visit. Our parents had fallen ill at the time, so I assumed your mother had come down with you to check in on them. However, the moment she stepped from the carriage, I knew something was amiss. The skin around her eyes had that sleepless swell, and tears fell down her cheeks as soon as she met my gaze. That was when she told me the tragic news. The men had been traveling through some rough terrain on their business trip. The weather turned poor and the wheels on the carriage holding your father and grandfather had come loose. The carriage skidded through the mud, right over a steep cliff. Neither man was able to exit the carriage in time and both . . . perished in the fall."

"They died together?"

Fidelia nodded. "Your uncle was on his way back home as your mother received the news via telegram. I remember she showed me the message. August had expressed his deepest condolences and assured her that he would have saved them if it had been possible."

"Why did Uncle refuse to tell me this story?" Hestia asked hesitantly, as if she knew the answer but refused to face it.

"Perhaps the grief and pain it brings him to recall it is too much. However, there could be another reason, one your mother suspected until the very end. Your mother—the grief over two such sudden losses not only destroyed her spirit but it also made her suspect the absolute worst. Helena believed that August's jealousy had finally gotten the better of him and that he must have tampered with the wheels on the carriage, which sent it over the cliff's edge."

Hestia's eyes widened. "She believed he . . . killed them?"

"There was very little that could scare your mother, but Hestia, I will never forget the look on her face that day at our cottage. I never saw her look so helpless and so . . . utterly terrified."

"What did you do when my mother confessed this to you?"

"There was very little I *could* do. From the day we met, I felt that there was always something a bit off about August. However, to suppose that anyone would stoop to something so wicked, I was conflicted. On the one hand, I wanted to stand by my sister no matter what. But on the other, I could not wrap my head around an act so vile. I simply encouraged Helena to stay at the cottage with me until August returned home, but she refused. Even in moments of great terror, your mother was steadfast. Nonetheless, she did request that I keep you at the cottage until August returned, which I happily agreed to do. I held you in my arms as her carriage carried her away toward the manor . . . and that was the very last time I ever saw my sister."

Hestia gasped. "So, you never saw or spoke to her after that day?"

Fidelia shook her head. "The next morning, a carriage pulled up, and a short, stocky woman stepped out and requested that I hand you over to her. She said that she had come at the request of Lord Rosewood to collect the baby."

"Jessamine . . ."

"Yes. I tried to keep you, to inquire as to my sister's whereabouts, but Jessamine knew very little. She did assure me, however, that you would be safe. So, I handed you over to her, and I never saw you again until that day you entered your uncle's study not too long ago."

"Didn't you ever try to visit us?"

"I wanted to, believe me," Fidelia said. "But I was my parents' sole caregiver. I *did* write, but things only turned worse as those letters went unanswered. Before I knew it, one year had gone by since I'd had any contact with Helena. No carriages came near our cottage. The stipends and food that had been sustaining us from the manor stopped, with no explanation. Soon, there was no money left and our parents' health worsened until they at last passed away, shortly before my nineteenth birthday. Until that point, I had assumed that grief and fear had kept your mother away, though I was sure that the death of our parents would be enough to reunite us. So, when your mother never came, nor responded to my letter, I felt that something was very wrong. But still, there was nothing I could do. As a penniless, unmarried woman with nowhere else to turn, I entered a local workhouse in London. It was here, nearly one year later, where I overheard one of the other ladies mention a 'tragic death at Deston Manor' during a session of idle gossip. I assumed they were referring to your father or grandfather, until I heard one of them say something about a fair blonde woman. It was then that I knew your mother was no longer with us."

Hestia's blood ran cold.

"A part of me died the day I learned that your mother, my beloved sister, was gone. And that same day, all resistance to your mother's beliefs about your uncle left me completely. Many believed that grief had led Helena to take her own life. But I knew my sister. No matter what turmoil she faced, she would not have allowed it to control her. And she would not have willingly left you. So, I replayed those conversations with your mother in my head. The advances, the leering, the rages. I began to piece together a story that, once complete, shook me and made me determined to find and rescue you."

"What was it?" Hestia inquired.

"Hestia, it has taken me years to come to terms with the words I am about to say, but after sharing my story with you, I dare say I believe it more than ever. Your uncle, August, is a murderer."

CHAPTER NINE

Fidelia's statement echoed with a shrill ring in Hestia's ears. *Is it true? Could Uncle really . . .* The girl's mind wouldn't allow her to finish the thought that brewed at the very edge of her consciousness. In a moment of sudden clarity, she began piecing together memories from her recurring dream. "My dream," Hestia whispered.

"Hestia?" Fidelia inquired.

"My recurring dream, the one I told you about. I wonder if it has something to do with my mother and father. It always begins the same, with a man and a woman whose faces I can never quite make out. They are standing at an altar, and the man grabs the woman's wrists. Then, the woman—"

"Screams? Hestia, in this dream, does the woman's dress turn blood red?"

Hestia nodded.

"And are both of these figures then locked away behind a pale-blue door?"

Goosebumps appeared on Hestia's skin.

"I have been having that same dream ever since I stepped through the threshold of this manor," Fidelia said. "Only, in *my* dream, I can clearly see the man and woman, as if they were standing before me now."

"Who are they, Aunt Delia?" Hestia asked, as if the answer was not already manifesting as a lump at the base of her throat.

"They are your uncle and your mother."

Tears began to well in Hestia's eyes.

Fidelia, sensing her distress, pulled her close. "I am sorry that these dark visions have plagued you for so long," Fidelia said, stroking the girl's hair.

"Why?" Hestia muffled the simple question into her aunt's torso.

"Your uncle is a callous, jealous, and covetous man. And based on my unease with him upon our first meeting, I venture that he may have always been that way. I cannot be sure of your grandfather's true intentions, Hestia, but I believe that he could sense that something inside your uncle was a bit broken. I am sure that when he decided to pass his legacy to your father, he thought he was doing what was best to preserve the Rosewood name. However, what he did instead was breed an unchecked contempt. And the more I replay those conversations with your mother in my head, the more I also realize that it was not only the Rosewood legacy that August envied your father for, but your mother herself. I would not be surprised to learn that your uncle tried to court Helena upon Jonathan's death, only for her to reject his advances."

"You believe that Uncle was in love with my mother?"

"Yes. Most men who saw your mother fell headfirst, and the look on August's face the day he and Jonathan met your mother and I should have served as my first warning. I only wish I would have had the foresight to know what would become of his actions."

"Do you believe that Uncle intends to bring me harm?"

Fidelia sighed. "I am not sure. Your previous remark on his rages proves that his temperament hasn't altered much from when your mother was alive. It may only be a matter of time before he becomes dangerous again."

"How did you manage to conjure this plan to save me, Aunt Delia? To pose as my new governess and infiltrate the manor?"

"Well, after the initial shock of your mother's death wore off, I kept my ears open and finally heard that you were indeed still alive, and well, at least as well as you could be. That same night, I awoke in a cold sweat from the most vivid dream. I was back in the room Helena and I shared in our parents' cottage. Your mother, as young and beautiful as I remembered her, appeared before me and implored me to save you. I will never forget the exact words, as they haunt me to this day: 'You could not save me, but you *will* save her.' From that day forward, I thought up countless schemes to find my way into the manor. Unfortunately, I never found the courage or time to bring any of them to fruition. Days grew into weeks, weeks into months, and months into years, and while Helena's words never left me, I began to lose all hope. Before I knew it, nearly twelve years had passed. Luck did not look my way again until only months ago. I was collecting the washing one evening, and out of the corner of my eye, I spotted movement. When I turned, I saw an unknown figure dropping some parchments by the workhouse door. Before I could approach the figure to inquire as to their identity, they ran off. When I picked up one of the parchments that had been dropped, I saw it was an advertisement seeking a governess for the fifteen-year-old niece of one Lord August Rosewood. I knew this would be my shining opportunity, so I stashed the other parchments away so no one else would see the open position and immediately set a plan into motion to volunteer."

Fidelia reached behind her and pulled out the workhouse record that had been taken from her. She pointed to Priscilla's name. "Priscilla Evans was a close friend of mine. She and I were the same age, and I had shared many of my stories, thoughts, and suspicions with her over the years. One week prior to receiving the advertisement, Priscilla had succumbed to scarlet fever. When I realized I would need an alias, I decided to carry her name as my own as a way to honor her. I ripped this page and the one with my name from the workhouse record book and altered them to erase Fidelia Ward from existence. As far as anyone knows from reading those books, there never was a Fidelia Ward in the workhouse. Only Priscilla Evans, who left a few days ago to begin a new position as governess to a noble family."

Both women sat in silence, taking a moment to breathe and absorb the night's revelations.

"Can we run away?" Hestia whispered.

"As much as I wish we could, your uncle has too many connections. We would be quickly found. Our only hope is to find incontrovertible evidence that points to my suspicions. Once we have this, we can bring August to justice, and you will be set free from his grasp."

"If we find this evidence and I am finally untethered from him, where will I go?"

"You and I will find a way to survive." Fidelia took her niece's small hand in her own. "Now that I have found you again, I do not endeavor to leave you. Fate has brought us together for a reason, and I intend to see that reason through."

"So, what now?"

"Are there any areas of the manor that have been closed off to you? Areas that August has forbidden you from? Those areas may hold exactly what we need to reveal the truth."

"Yes. He has never allowed me to visit the second-floor chambers. And his bookshelf. He has never permitted me to uncover what is under the damask sheet he hangs over its one side."

"I remember that shelf. Perhaps we should start small and make that our first target. We will just need the perfect time of day to enter his study without arousing suspicion."

"Lunch should be suitable," Hestia replied, a bit too quickly. "That is when we snuck into your room. Jessamine was never the wiser."

"*We*?" Fidelia questioned.

Hestia sheepishly looked at her feet. "Yes, I forgot to mention that I may have had some . . . assistance with retrieving those items from your sleeping quarters."

"Who?"

"Ezekiel."

"The gardener's son?"

Hestia nodded.

Fidelia sighed. "Moving forward, I would suggest that as few people as possible be involved in this. Any interference from outside parties could jeopardize everything and put you in harm's way. And that is the last thing I wish to do. Do you understand me?"

"Yes, Aunt Delia."

"This Ezekiel, is he special to you?"

"Special? Well, I have not known him for long, but he is very kind." A smile spread across her face as she thought of him. "He was scared of what he was risking by helping me. But still, he followed through."

"He knew it was important to you," Fidelia surmised. "It sounds like he may be enamored with you, Hestia."

"Perhaps, but I suppose we are not . . . socially compatible."

Fidelia leaned in closer. "I know that our relationship as aunt and niece is quite new, but if I may offer a piece of advice: society will always dictate what is and is not acceptable. But your heart dictates what does and does not bring you true happiness. You can choose to follow the former and live a life of acceptability, or you can follow your heart and live a life of happiness."

"My mother and father followed their hearts, and we both know where it led them."

"Mark me, Hestia. Your mother and father *did* live a life of true happiness together. Just because it was short does not mean it was any less filled with joy and love." The two women smiled at that irrefutable certainty. "Now, on to the details of our plan. The sooner we can begin to uncover the truth, the better. I suggest that we set everything in motion this coming afternoon by exploring your uncle's study."

"But how will we get in? Uncle takes his keys with him when he leaves, and I cannot very well ask Jessamine for hers."

Fidelia gave Hestia a sly look. "While I will admit that I am not proud of this fact, I *did* happen to pick up lock picking while in the workhouse. I—" Just then, the clocks in the hall chimed three times. "I didn't realize it was so late," Fidelia said, standing up. "I am sorry for keeping you awake so long, my dear."

"It is quite alright, Aunt Delia. I dare say our conversation this evening was far worth a bit of exhaustion in the morning." Quickly and quietly, Hestia led Fidelia to her chamber door.

"Meet me at your uncle's study tomorrow afternoon," Fidelia whispered.

"I will," Hestia replied. "I will just need to get things sorted with Jessamine. But I will be there."

With that, Fidelia slowly opened the door, slipping out and heading toward her sleeping quarters.

Both women were in such a state of excitement that neither had heard the soft footsteps retreat away from Hestia's door. Nor had they heard the slight creak of the door to August's study as it opened and a dark figure slid inside. And neither heard the door open and shut once more as the figure left the study ten minutes later, a piece of parchment in hand.

CHAPTER TEN

The next morning arrived far too soon as Hestia awoke to the firm touch of a hand shaking her.

"Up and at 'em, dearie!" Jessamine pulled the bed sheets away from Hestia, exposing the young girl to the air of the room. As Hestia came to, she noticed Jessamine flitting about with an unusually nervous energy.

What has Jessamine so excited this morning? Hestia thought. "Jessamine, is everything alright? You seem a bit agitated this morning."

"Oh, I'm just fine, dearie. It's just . . ." Jessamine ceased her erratic movements and turned to Hestia. "How have you and Ms. Evans been getting on?"

"We are getting along just fine, Jessamine. Why?" Hestia turned away from her handmaiden and bit her lip.

"Good, that's good, dearie. I just want to make sure that Ms. Evans is treating you agreeably. Sometimes, manor staff can forget their place and start speaking out of turn, especially when they're around someone who they think might listen to them."

"Well, Ms. Evans has been treating me quite alright, Jessamine. Trust me, if something was off about her, I wouldn't keep it to myself." Hestia hated lying to her handmaiden, but knew it was necessary to avoid any other parties growing suspicious.

Jessamine walked back in front of Hestia, forcing her to face her. The handmaiden set down a pot, took both of Hestia's hands, and leaned in closer, until their noses were mere inches apart. "Just mind yourself around her, dearie. Every now and then, those we trust only seek to twist our minds to meet their own agendas." Both women stared at each intently before Jessamine, as if broken from a trance, abruptly dropped Hestia's hands and picked up the pot, leaving the room.

When she returned a moment later, she had fresh water for Hestia. "I'm sorry to be speaking so boldly this morning. I just worry about you. I have cared for you since you were three years old," Jessamine said. "You are like a daughter to me."

Hestia thought of Fidelia's story, when Jessamine came to collect Hestia as a toddler, leaving her aunt alone and helpless. *How much did Jessamine know at that time? How much does she know now?*

"Just know that if anything happens, you can always come to me," Jessamine said.

"Thank you, Jessamine," Hestia replied. "I will endeavor to remember that."

The two began to prepare for the day ahead. As Jessamine pulled the last tie on Hestia's corset, she heard a light rapping at the chamber door.

"Yes?" Jessamine cracked the chamber door open and was met by Fidelia, or Ms. Evans, as the handmaiden still knew her to be.

"Good morning, Jessamine. Can you please let Lady Rosewood know that we will be unable to meet for our morning lesson? Unfortunately, the weakened state I was in yesterday prevented me from preparing the appropriate lesson plan. I will need today to make up for lost time."

"Of course, Ms. Evans," Jessamine said. "I do hope you are feeling much better today. Forgive me for saying so, but a woman with delicate features such as yours should be getting as much rest as possible to fend off those *weakened states*."

The last two words fell out of Jessamine's mouth in such a precise tone that Fidelia stared at the handmaiden for a moment before flashing her a nervous smile. "Thank you, Jessamine," Fidelia finally squeaked out before taking her leave.

"Who was that, Jessamine?" Hestia inquired.

"It seems that Ms. Evans won't be meeting with you this morning, dearie. Your wonderful governess neglected to prepare a lesson plan for today."

Hestia was sure that Fidelia was preparing for their afternoon escapades, but the sarcasm that dripped off of Jessamine's tongue left her concerned that the handmaiden may be growing more perceptive than expected. "Oh, well I am sure I can find a way to pass the time before lunch."

Once dressed, Hestia made her way to the drawing room where she told Jessamine she would be practicing her sewing. In reality, she paced the room for hours as thoughts of the past and prospects of the future played in her mind. Finally, she looked at the clock and saw the noon hour drawing near. In an effort to avoid raising further suspicion, she grabbed her sewing and threw together some rough stitches before Jessamine came to fetch her.

"Let me see, I suppose you are going to want to eat outside today?" Jessamine inquired, glancing out the drawing room window.

"Whatever would give you that idea?"

"I've already got Hiram getting everything prepared," Jessamine responded as they shuffled out of the room and began to walk down the hall. "I may actually join you for a bit. I've been meaning to give the grounds a good once-over while Lord Rosewood is away. Besides, this weather may do me some good."

Panic flooded Hestia's mind, though she endeavored not to expose herself to Jessamine. "Are you quite sure you have the time, Jessamine? After all, Adella may need your help inside. Remember the last time you left her to do the washing? My white petticoat is still tinged a lovely shade of rose."

"I think Adella will manage just fine on her own for a while. Now, why don't we head on out?" Jessamine turned toward the kitchen to retrieve the supplies for lunch. Hestia followed slowly behind, her thoughts swirling with potential schemes to wriggle herself free from Jessamine's watchful eye.

Lunch in hand, the two women then made their way to the manor's doors. The clocks already marked the time at 12:05. Only ten more minutes until Hestia would be expected outside of her uncle's study. *If only a miracle would occur.*

As quickly as this thought entered her mind, the pair stepped outside and Hestia caught sight of Ezekiel tending to the shrubs nearest the back entrance. *Ask and ye shall receive,* Hestia thought with a grin.

"Lady Rosewood, Ms. Jessamine." Ezekiel bowed.

"Hello, Ezekiel," Jessamine said. "How is your father?"

"Oh, he is doing as well as he can. No better, but no worse."

"Well, thank God for that," Jessamine said.

As Ezekiel and Jessamine exchanged pleasantries, Hestia stole glances at the young man. Trying to time it perfectly, she waited for the right time to interject. "Jessamine! Weren't you telling me the other day how you would love to speak with Ezekiel and his father about some of your landscaping ideas?"

Jessamine looked at Hestia in surprise. "Well, yes, but—"

"So, why don't you while we are out here? I am sure Ezekiel wouldn't mind, would you?"

Ezekiel shot Hestia a confused expression until he caught a pleading one from her. "Um, yes, that would be fine, Ms. Jessamine," Ezekiel replied. "Actually, my father still leads the landscaping plans. I just carry out whatever he has the energy to come up with. He should be almost done with lunch, if you'd like to speak with him at our cottage." Ezekiel pointed her in the direction of the Miller cottage, which lay just outside of the manor grounds.

"I really shouldn't," Jessamine said. "I wouldn't want to intrude on your father's lunch hour."

"Come now, Jessamine, I'm sure it will be fine," Hestia said, gently shoving Jessamine toward the cottage.

"If I didn't know any better, I'd say you're trying to get rid of me, dearie," Jessamine replied.

Hestia's eyes widened in mock surprise. "Now, why on earth would I want to be rid of you? I just know that gardening has always been a passion of yours and that you deserve to have your wonderful ideas known."

Jessamine eyed Hestia suspiciously.

Why is Jessamine so keen on being around me today? Hestia did her best to mask her unease with a smile.

"Well," Jessamine began, looking toward the Miller cottage. "Alright. But you—" Jessamine pointed at Ezekiel. "I know you have work of your own, so I expect you to do it. But could you also do me a favor and make sure that Hestia eats her lunch? If anything, or *anyone*, comes by to get in the way of that, you come get me."

"Of course, ma'am," Ezekiel said with a bow.

"Great." Now, turning to Hestia, she said, "I will be back at one o'clock. Please eat your lunch."

"Yes, Jessamine," Hestia agreed, taking the lunch basket from the handmaiden.

Jessamine headed toward the cottage and the two watched carefully until Jessamine's figure was no longer in view.

"Ezekiel, you must help me!" Hestia whispered excitedly. "I don't have much time, but there is so much I need to tell you!" Suddenly, the young woman took off, jogging back toward the manor.

Ezekiel stared after her until he saw her gesture for him to follow. He did as he was told, and the two raced, Hestia only stopping once to drop the basket at her table. Finally, the two reached the manor's front entrance.

"Hestia, what is going on? Why is Jessamine acting so odd? And what about your lunch?"

"I don't know what's got Jessamine in such a tizzy today, and my lunch can wait. The girl in the photograph, it's her."

"Your mother?" Ezekiel questioned.

"No, well, yes, but the other girl. The dark haired one. *That* is Ms. Evans. Only her given name is Fidelia Ward. She is my aunt." Hestia briefly recapped the highlights of the revelations she received from Fidelia the night before, including her suspicions of August's nefarious behavior.

As she wrapped her tale, Ezekiel's eyes darted side to side, processing all that had been said. He shook his head before he spoke again. "I-I don't know what to say except . . . Hestia, if your uncle really plans to bring you harm like your aunt thinks, then I am willing to do anything I can to help."

Hestia flashed a warm smile at Ezekiel that made the young man's stomach flip. "I do not wish to put you in harm's way more than I already have, but you can act as my lookout. Aunt Delia is waiting for me just outside my uncle's study. We are going to break in and see if we can find evidence to support my aunt's beliefs. While we are inside, I ask that you keep a watchful eye for Jessamine's return. I will try to be back before one o'clock."

"Wait, if I see Jessamine coming, how should I signal to you?"

"Good question . . ." Hestia contemplated this for a moment. "There is a window to Uncle's study on the manor's right side. It is the only first-floor window on that side. If you see Jessamine coming, run to the side and knock on the window twice. That will signal to us that she is on her way."

"I can do that," Ezekiel said.

Hestia briefly wrapped her arms around Ezekiel in thanks. "I am most indebted to you, Ezekiel. I hope you know that."

"Anytime, Hestia. I mean that."

The pair released their hug, and Hestia quickly and quietly pushed the doors of the manor open. She waved as she stepped through the threshold and closed the doors behind her. Looking down, she pondered for a moment if she should remove her shoes, as she and Ezekiel had done during their first investigation. Jessamine was not there, but Adella still posed a potential threat.

Suddenly, the memory of Adella's note flashed through Hestia's mind. *"I'd suggest you both move quickly."* Adella knew more than she let on and clearly did not seem to be in a rush to tell someone. So, intent to waste no more time, Hestia left her shoes on and scampered down the hall toward her uncle's study.

"Cutting it a bit close," Fidelia remarked upon Hestia's arrival.

"I know. I had a minor issue with Jessamine, but it is resolved now. On to the task at hand."

Fidelia removed a pin from her hair and plugged it into the study's door lock. Hestia watched in fascination as Fidelia jiggled the pin, her ear pressed against the wood. "Ah," Fidelia said after a few moments. "Just the sound I was hoping for." She smiled at her niece, pulled the pin out, and pushed the door open, revealing the study.

"You must teach me that sometime," Hestia said in amazement.

Gingerly, the two women stepped through the threshold of the study and closed the door behind them. The room was encased in a musty darkness, and both women fumbled through the space as they tried to find a source of light. Hestia's hand met one of the thick curtains, and she started to pull it back before she heard a sharp intake of breath.

"Better we keep those closed," Fidelia said. Whether it was simple paranoia or experience informing her aunt's decision, Hestia was unsure. Yet, she felt it best not to question as she let the curtain fall back to its original state. Fidelia, meanwhile, reached August's desk and managed to find a set of matches in one of his drawers.

"There should be a lamp on his desk," Hestia said.

Fidelia felt around until she found it. Hestia watched as a small flame appeared and entered the lamp, illuminating the room. August's study always had a foreboding presence in Hestia's life, but on this day, it felt especially menacing. The tightly shut windows cut off all sense of light and air in the room, suffocating the space. The desk sat in the center, anxiously awaiting the return of its owner. The bookcase stood tall and proud, its gray damask sheet hanging limply across titles that had been forbidden from Hestia's sight, until today.

"That's the one." Goosebumps erupted on Hestia's arms as the prospect of what she may find swam through her mind. *What secrets lay in wait? What untold stories stood like ghosts just waiting to be seen?*

Both women stepped toward the covered bookcase with ritualistic care, as if the weight of the very world rested behind that old sheet. "I will pull the sheet back," Fidelia said, reaching a hand out. With deliberate care, she lifted it, at last revealing the tomes that lay beneath.

Hestia and Fidelia gazed at the full collection of books exposed before them. While the uncovered side of the shelf saw many typical titles of the time, this new side held books that Hestia had never known to exist before. A full compendium of poisons. A grimoire of black magick. Books on murder, jealousy, rage, and other treacherous topics. For every profane and perverted activity in which one could participate, August's bookshelf had a title for it.

"If this isn't proof enough of your suspicions, I don't know what will be," Hestia exclaimed.

"What is that?" Fidelia pointed toward an older book on the shelf.

Hestia pulled the book from its place and carried it over to August's desk before peering inside. "It looks like the Rosewood family tree," Hestia said.

Fidelia dropped the sheet back down and joined Hestia at the desk. Hestia explored the page before her, seeing, for the first time, the great lineage of Rosewoods who had come before her. As she approached the bottom of the tree, her brow furrowed. Under the name of Hestia's paternal grandfather, Thaddeus, she saw both her father and uncle's names. Only her uncle's name appeared to be in a different handwriting, while her father's name had a crude arrow drawn next to it, connecting it to a man listed next to Thaddeus—Eli Rosewood.

"This looks like Uncle's handwriting here," Hestia noted, pointing to August's entry.

As they continued to follow the tree, they saw next to Jonathan's name was another name that had been crossed out. Though they couldn't make out much, a soft "H" gave them the clue they needed to solve the riddle.

"Why would my mother's name be crossed out?" Hestia inquired.

"Hestia, look here."

Hestia followed her aunt's finger, which pointed to the margins of the tree just outside of where August's name sat. There, both women saw Helena's name scrawled in August's penmanship. "Why would Uncle place my mother's name next to his? Unless . . ." Suddenly, aspects of Hestia's recurring dream stabbed at her mind like a knife. The white rose awning. The white dress. A man and a woman. *'Til death do us part.* "Aunt Delia, do you think that Uncle married my mother?"

"I can't imagine that she would've accepted his hand. Unless he . . . threatened her."

Hestia could hear the blood rushing through her ears as she stared blankly at the tree before her. If August had loved her mother enough to develop an elaborate plan to get rid of her father and marry her, then why would he turn around and kill her as well? This thought bit at Hestia as she continued to study the tree. She followed it to her own name, written with a much more proper hand than the one her uncle possessed. However, she did notice that August had drawn a crude arrow pointing from her name to his own. As she followed the arrow, she saw a note across the margin that read: Revise after wedding.

Hestia's hands went numb. "Aunt Delia, what does this mean?" With a shaky finger, she pointed at her discovery.

Fidelia leaned in closer, letting out a small gasp when she read the words.

"Uncle never wanted me to leave this manor," Hestia began, pieces falling into place within her mind. "He never allowed me to interact with others my own age, and he told me that there were certain duties I would be taking on as a member of the family." Hestia could feel herself growing hysterical as the reality of August's true plan washed over her.

"Hestia, look at me," Fidelia said, gripping her shoulders.

Tears formed in Hestia's eyes. "Uncle plans to ma—"

"Hestia, whatever your uncle has planned will not happen. It *cannot* happen. It is not legal."

"We are talking about a man who you say murdered my parents. I hardly think legalities are an issue to him."

Fidelia gripped her niece's shoulders to quell her shaking. "Whatever your uncle plans to do with you will not happen. I promise you that." She looked her niece straight in the eye before glancing at the clock. "It is nearly one. We must be getting you back before Jessamine catches us. You said there was another part of the manor that August forbade you from, correct?"

"Aunt Delia, I—"

"Correct?"

"The second-floor chambers," the girl whispered.

"Then we shall prepare to explore those tomorrow." Fidelia released her grip on Hestia and closed the book containing the family tree. She placed it back in its place on the bookcase and pulled the damask sheet to ensure it was left as they had found it. Fidelia blew out the lamp on August's desk before they exited the room, the older woman ensuring that the door locked as it closed.

Fidelia followed Hestia to the front door and grasped her hand tightly before letting her go. "No matter what may happen from this point on, know that I love you."

"I love you, too, Aunt Delia," Hestia replied.

With that, Hestia raced out the door to her seat in the garden. On the way, she nodded at Ezekiel, permitting him to drop his watch and return to his work. Despite recent revelations making her nearly sick to her stomach, Hestia crammed her lunch into her mouth just as Jessamine made her way back up from the Miller cottage.

"Are you ready to head back inside, dearie?" Jessamine said as she approached Hestia.

"Oh, yes, Jessamine," Hestia replied, the last bit of food still trapped in her teeth. "How did your meeting with Mr. Miller go?"

"Very well. I think Lord Rosewood will be quite pleased with the new landscaping plans." Jessamine began to prattle on about her meeting with Ambrose as she led Hestia back inside the manor.

The girl only half-listened, her mind too consumed with the implications of the afternoon's findings and what other secrets lay in wait.

"Dearie, are you feeling alright? You look a little peaky," Jessamine said, finally taking note of Hestia's appearance.

"I think the sun may have been too much for me today, Jessamine. I think I am going to lay down for a bit."

The handmaiden led Hestia back to her bedchamber, and as they passed Fidelia's quarters, Hestia cast a glance toward the closed door. A sudden tightness pervaded her chest as she considered all she now knew, as opposed to the naivete she possessed when she and Ezekiel first stood outside that door.

Both Hestia and Fidelia slept through the rest of the day, only waking long enough to partake in a quiet supper. They exchanged glances across the table as they ate, taking care to turn away when Jessamine was in sight. Both then decided to turn in early, still exhausted from the day.

It would be for the best, they would learn, as they would need every measure of their faculties about them to face what came next. For as night faded and the sun rose over another day at Deston Manor, Jessamine heard a rapping at the main door. She answered it to find a messenger with a telegram. She thanked him and eagerly accepted the note. Closing the door behind her, her eyes devoured the message that lay before her:

Jessamine,

As you read this missive, I am already on my way home. I shall arrive by Thursday evening. Ensure that supper is prepared and that the girl and her governess are present. You may join us as well, but no one else.

Thank you for your note. We will have much to discuss.

-A.R.

CHAPTER ELEVEN

The shock of the previous day's revelations had utterly worn Hestia to the bone. When Jessamine came in the next morning, Hestia was nearly impossible to stir, and when she finally did, the state of her convinced Jessamine to let her rest a bit longer. She did not end up opening her eyes again until it was almost noon, and only then because she recalled her plan to meet with Fidelia.

"Are you sure you're alright, dearie?" Jessamine said as she came to collect Hestia for lunch. "It's not like you to need so much sleep."

"I will be fine, Jessamine," Hestia reassured. "I just think all of the fresh air I have been getting is catching up with me."

"Just as long as you're ready for supper tonight. It is a special one, and I wouldn't want you missing it on account of being ill."

A special one? As Jessamine helped her dress and prepare for the afternoon, Hestia allowed this question to join the stew of fear, anger, and hopelessness that plagued her mind. *Hestia Rosewood, new bride to the great Lord August Rosewood.* The thought alone conjured a taste of bile in her mouth. While logic could argue up until that point that the accusations of Hestia's aunt and mother made little case for persecution, Hestia could not shake the truth she herself had seen.

Following a brief lunch, she and Fidelia resumed the formalities of their lessons. They did manage to sneak in a brief conversation regarding their next investigation which, due to their late start, would have to wait until that night when the servants were in bed. As afternoon wore into evening, the pair wrapped up their lesson for the day and went their separate ways to prepare for supper.

Hestia sat still and silent on her bed, endless thoughts consuming her as she waited for Jessamine to fetch her for dinner.

The handmaiden was making her way down the hall to Hestia's bedchamber when she heard a *clicking* on the cobble-stones just outside of the manor. As Jessamine peered out the window, she caught a glimpse of a carriage coming up the pathway and rushed to Hestia's room. "Dearie, it is time for supper."

I don't know if I can face another meal in silence, Hestia thought. "I am sorry, Jessamine, but I think I may be coming down with something after all. Perhaps I could take my supper in he—"

"No."

Hestia started at Jessamine's harsh response.

"I apologize, dearie," Jessamine softened. "What I mean is, I told you we were having a special meal tonight, and I think it would do you some good to come out and join us."

"Us?"

"Yes, I will be joining you and Ms. Evans tonight," Jessamine said with a smile. "Come on, now. You can't just stay in bed with nothing to eat."

Relenting, Hestia followed Jessamine down the hall. As the two walked, Hestia noticed that her handmaiden appeared to be in a peculiarly chipper mood. "You seem unusually excited, Jessamine." She had the strangest feeling that Jessamine knew something she didn't.

"Nonsense. I am just looking forward to our meal. It is not every day a servant gets to eat with the masters of the house."

Wait—Masters of the house?

As the two neared the dining room, Hestia could not seem to shake a feeling of unease that gripped at the edges of her mind. Jessamine seemed a bit *too* excited about such a simple affair as supper, and it wasn't until she paid attention that Hestia sensed an odd and sudden shift in the energy of the manor. Whether a trick of her mind or not, the feeling followed her as the pair entered the dining room's threshold.

Jessamine practically skipped into the room and turned to welcome Hestia inside. The young girl crossed the threshold and first made eye contact with her aunt. Fidelia was sitting directly in front of her, eyes wide and mouth tightly pursed, as if bound to remain shut. Hestia stepped forward and was just about to address her aunt when a figure at the very end of the table caught her peripheral vision.

"Hello, my dear niece."

Turning, Hestia came face-to-face with a pair of unmistakable, intense gray eyes. Her heart fell into her stomach, and it took every ounce of courage within her to utter a reply. "Uncle, you're home."

CHAPTER TWELVE

Hestia stared down the table at the chair that held her uncle, the silence stinging her ears. Seconds passed like hours until, at last, August gestured to the chair next to him. "Come, have a seat."

"Uncle, I—"

"Sit," August ordered.

Reluctantly, Hestia obeyed, sliding into the chair next to her uncle and fighting the tremors that threatened to overtake her body. As soon as she settled herself, she looked around the room. All color that had remained in Fidelia's countenance was completely gone, while Jessamine shot Hestia a reassuring smile. Hestia could hear Jessamine's voice in her head: "Everything will be alright now. Lord Rosewood is home."

"Hestia, would you say that I have provided for you?"

"Uncle?"

"Have I not provided you with every comfort and every opportunity that you have desired?"

"You have provided me with shelter, food, and education," Hestia countered.

"Have you ever wanted for any material possession that I did not secure for you?" August questioned.

"I suppose not."

"Then, why is it that you seek to destroy me?"

Both Hestia and Fidelia glanced at each other before turning their eyes back to August, who rose from his seat and sauntered toward the dining room window.

"You have not asked why I am home early, niece," August said, facing the window.

"Why are you home early, Uncle?" Hestia asked, unsure where this conversation was heading but already fearing the consequences.

August smiled under his breath. "Such a foolish girl. Did you never stop to think that I would have someone trusted here who could report to me while I was away? Someone who would warn me if events began to transpire outside of my control? I must admit I expected you to possess more common sense than that." As August uttered those final words, he turned his eyes toward the handmaiden.

Hestia followed this movement and instantly recalled her odd conversation with Jessamine the morning before. Her eyes widened as realization swept over her. "Jessamine?" Hestia said. "Did you tell Uncle something to make him come home early?"

"I'm sorry, dearie," Jessamine admitted. "But I couldn't just stand by and let that woman put such unnatural thoughts into your head."

"And what unnatural thoughts have I to share?" Fidelia asked.

"*You* will not speak unless given permission to do so," August barked, pointing a long finger at Fidelia.

Fidelia flashed him an amused smirk. "What's wrong, August? Does my defiance remind you of someone?"

August's eyes sparked with rage as he stared down the governess. He allowed a sharp exhale to escape gritted teeth before reluctantly dropping the matter for the moment.

"What do you think you know, Jessamine?" Hestia questioned.

"Oh, I know enough," Jessamine said, turning sharp eyes onto Fidelia. "I know that this woman is not who she said she is and that she tried to put some ridiculous story into your poor, innocent head. So, I decided to put an end to it before it got any worse. I was only trying to look out for you, dearie. You and Lord Rosewood."

At that moment, August smiled and walked over to Jessamine's seat. As he placed a protective hand upon Jessamine's shoulder, Hestia and Fidelia looked at each other nervously. "Yes, Hestia, Jessamine was simply protecting what she knows to be most important. She was proving her loyalty to us and to this great manor. I must say, I am surprised that you would not show more gratitude to the woman who practically raised you all of these years."

Hestia's eyes shifted once more toward her aunt.

August caught this brief moment and scoffed. "So, it *is* true. Jessamine suspected that you may have been falling under the spell of this wretch's tales, which is why I saw fit to come home early. But even as I sat in my carriage, a speck of my heart assured me that my darling niece would never believe the words of a stranger over the comfort that her loving uncle has provided her all these years." August stepped closer to Hestia, sending a tremor up her spine. "But perhaps that speck of my heart was misguided."

"It wouldn't be the first time your judgment clouded your actions, from what I hear." The words rolled off of Hestia's tongue with such ease that she surprised even herself.

August's eyes bore into Hestia's. "So, what exactly did Ms. Ward tell you about me?"

"Enough," Hestia began. "Enough to suspect that you are not the kind and caring uncle you believe you are in your mind. And enough to inspire an investigation that, let's just say, proved to be rather illuminating."

"I see," August said, turning to Fidelia. "And where did this investigation take place?"

"Your study." Hestia said the words slowly in an attempt to keep her voice from shaking. "I saw what lay beneath the sheet on your bookcase. Such ghastly titles. And, of course, the family tree."

Jessamine's brow furrowed, and August's face fell at these final words. "You found the family tree?" he questioned.

Hestia nodded. "And your . . . revisions." For the first time all day, Hestia could feel her confidence return as she stared her uncle down.

His eyes flashed with rage as he released a shaky breath. "How . . ." August began through gritted teeth. "How did you gain access to my study while I was away?"

"*I* assisted her," Fidelia replied this time. She proudly stood up from her seat and grasped her niece's hand.

August turned to Fidelia with an evil glare before facing Jessamine. "And you had no idea this was happening?"

Jessamine looked down at the table, guilt darkening her face. "No sir, I'm afraid I didn't, or I would have surely put a stop to it."

August let out a deep, frustrated sigh before pivoting his attention back to Hestia and Fidelia. "Well, I suppose you believe you have me all figured out, then," August said, relenting. "Yes, those books in my possession contain rather nefarious subjects, which is why I wished to hide them from your delicate sensibilities. I am a man of the world, so I must know every part of it, both light and dark. As for the family tree, it is true that I added some of my own revisions because I wished for the history of our family to be reflected accurately for future generations. My father and I shared a . . . complicated relationship, but I knew it would be up to me, as his only true son, to maintain honesty about who we are. The note about marriage was also—"

"*Only true son*?" Hestia interrupted.

Hestia, Fidelia, and Jesamine all looked at August with curiosity.

August paused as the realization of his slip sunk in. He walked toward the threshold of the dining room. "Well, my dear niece, if you wish so badly to know my secrets, then perhaps I should share them all." August gestured for Hestia to follow him. "Why don't we finish our conversation on the second floor?"

CHAPTER THIRTEEN

Four sets of eyes darted back and forth within the dining room as the three women stood dumbfounded. Once the implications of August's statement fully sunk in, Hestia timidly made her way toward her uncle. Fidelia and Jessamine rose to follow suit, but August raised his hand. "Hestia will come with me alone."

"Like hell she will," Fidelia bristled.

"Lord Rosewood," Jessamine began, attempting a lighter approach. "Please forgive me, sir. But I would very much appreciate the opportunity to accompany Lady Rosewood as well. As her handmaiden and head housekeeper of this manor, it is my responsibility to know all that I can about my charges, including their family's history."

Looking from Jessamine to Fidelia, August's face flashed a million emotions as he considered his options. Then, the three women noticed an unexpected glint appear in his eye. "Fine, you may both accompany us upstairs. But let us move quickly."

With that, the three women followed August out of the dining room and down the hallway leading to the staircase. Four hands gripped the railing as they carefully ascended the stairs. August forged ahead, silent and steadfast, with Hestia following behind, then Fidelia, and Jessamine bringing up the rear. Each step creaked and cracked, foretelling an uncertain doom that Hestia could feel in her bones. She looked back briefly as they climbed but could see no more proof of the ladies' presence than vague silhouettes. Suddenly, she felt a hand reach for her own and give it a reassuring squeeze. She smiled and turned around to continue the journey.

At last, the four approached the top of the stairs, which bled out into a large, dark hall. August confidently stepped forward and reached for a lamp that hung on the nearby wall. Pulling a match from his pocket, he lit the lamp and graced his company with some much-needed illumination. "This way," he announced.

The women gingerly traversed down the dimly lit hall behind him. The air was thick and musty, yet its scent felt strangely familiar to Hestia. The group passed August and Adella's bedchambers, which sat just across from each other at the front of the hall. Each step forward conjured another sense of deja-vu for the young woman as they approached the hallway's end. Finally, August stopped in front of a large door. It was evident from the peeling paint job that this door had been neglected for some time, a rather odd eyesore to be placed in such a stately manor as Deston. As Hestia leaned in to examine it closer, she made out a faint shade of pale-blue where the color remained, as well as a curiously shaped brown stain on the doorknob.

A pale-blue door. Suddenly, images from Hestia's recurring dream returned to her, and she let out a soft gasp.

"What is it?" Fidelia asked, immediately rushing to her side.

"The door in my dream. It was . . . a memory," Hestia whispered to her aunt before turning to address her uncle. "I have been here before."

"Hmm, I am surprised you would remember. You were quite young when you were last here." Without another moment's hesitation, he pulled a set of keys from his coat pocket and shifted them through his fingers until he found the one that he was seeking. Inserting the key into the lock, he gave it a turn until he heard it click. Gripping the knob, he then threw the door open, revealing the contents of the room within. "Ladies first." August gestured to the open threshold, eyes boring into those of his niece.

Taking a deep breath, Hestia entered the room, the other two women trailing behind her. In the twilight, Hestia could make out just enough to surmise that this room must have been a bedchamber in its former life. A small disheveled bed lay in the far-right corner, its posts adorned with cobwebs. What remained of a shattered vanity mirror sat near it, hiding its reflections beneath a film of dust. On the other side, a small crib stood across from the bed, the once white exterior now gray. Hestia walked around and closely surveyed the room. She pushed the rickety rocking chair that sat across from the crib, hearing its moan as if interrupted from a long slumber. Her hands danced across the wallpaper, torn and tarnished by the hands of time and fate. Finally, her eyes landed on the floorboards, where a large dark stain just near the bed's left side could be seen. "Every bit of this room, I can recall how it appeared when it was still new. But how?"

"I had hoped to never have to tell you this tale. Certain occurrences in life are best left unknown to such a delicate young woman, as I believed you to be. But now that I see you are so willing to disobey me as soon as I leave you with a taste of freedom, then I suppose it is time for you to understand the price of that decision." August began to pace the room as he prepared to launch into his tale. "Despite what you may have heard about me, Hestia, I am not a monster. Rather, I am a victim of circumstance. From the point of my very conception, I have had to claw my way to a place where I could receive the love, attention, and respect I deserved. My father, Thaddeus, was a cold, distant, and cruel man. He endeavored to keep me hidden away from society, a dirty secret that would blot the Rosewood family legacy. For so long, I wondered what I had done to deserve such harsh neglect. It was only after coming upon his journal shortly before his death that I received some form of an answer. For, you see, I was the result of an illicit affair that my father had with a local woman who everyone suspected to be a witch."

Hestia, Fidelia, and Jessamine's eyes widened at August's confession.

"Of course, when my father learned that the woman was pregnant, he immediately disowned both of us. However, it was only shortly after my birth when I landed on his doorstep. My mother, foolishly believing that a man who rejected me from the day of my conception would now accept me with open arms, left me with my father. To this day, I still wonder why he ever took me in, whether it was through fear or guilt. At any rate, I tried my best to be the son he wanted, even if I could not change my lineage. When I was about five years old, I thought that the tides were beginning to turn. My father started warming up to me, joining me for meals and the occasional walk in the garden. I believed that, at last, I would receive the affection I had craved for so long. And then, just one day shy of my sixth birthday, Jonathan Rosewood came to live with us." August watched the looks of confusion upon the three ladies and chuckled. "It is interesting that no one ever questioned my relationship with Jonathan, despite the fact that he and I looked nothing alike. The very idea that he was my brother was a pure fabrication by my father. In truth, he was the orphaned son of my father's brother, Eli. Upon the tragic passing of Eli and his wife, Jonathan was brought to my father."

Hestia looked into August's eyes and saw a sudden flash of rage that made her skin prickle.

"I did not understand it at the time, but now, I believe that my father saw Jonathan as an opportunity to begin anew, to raise a son who could properly carry out his legacy. All of the attention I had craved in those early years, the attention I finally began to receive, was taken from me overnight. From that day forward, my father pushed me further into the darkness instead, all while parading Jonathan around like a golden statue. Any love that I suspected my father was beginning to have for me had been usurped by Jonathan. Yes, I was still his son in name, still permitted to live in Deston Manor, but I was treated as a spare, while your *precious father* received all that should have been mine." August spat the last words in Hestia's direction.

Fidelia drew closer to her, clasping her hand around the young girl's. "Perhaps it was more than your lineage that your father did not like," Fidelia argued. "Perhaps he sensed something within you. Something . . . rotten."

"I am sorry that your father treated you so unfairly, but you speak as if my father intentionally stole him from you," Hestia said.

August looked from Fidelia to Hestia and revealed a wicked grin. "Oh, Jonathan did not steal my father from me, Hestia. He stole *everything* from me. That parchment that you found in my study has been in our family for decades. It is the duty of the Rosewood patriarch to keep our family tree up-to-date with each new birth, death, and marriage over the generations. When the time came for your grandfather to update the tree, I held a secret hope that he would see reason and finally bestow upon me the remorse, love, and blessings needed to carry out his legacy. But my father now had Jonathan, wonderful and noble Jonathan. He no longer required the existence of a bastard child like me. So, when he updated the tree, he took it upon himself to rewrite history entirely, removing me from existence and dropping Jonathan in my place." August paused and looked out the chamber's window, his memories getting the better of him. "There are only two other days after your father came to live with us that stand out as the worst of my life. The day your father was announced as the new Rosewood heir and the day he met your mother."

Fidelia shifted uncomfortably, fearing she would not be able to protect Hestia from what was about to come.

"You said that you know this room, Hestia, and you are correct. This room holds many memories, and one in particular that still haunts me to this day."

"What is this room, Uncle?" Hestia asked.

August gestured toward the old crib. "This room was your nursery, and the room in which your mother took her final breath."

CHAPTER FOURTEEN

August's words hung in the air like a bitter taste in Hestia's mouth. She surveyed the room around her, wondering just where in this space did the light leave her mother's eyes for the last time.

Her musings were not in vain, for luckily, August jumped quickly back into his side of the story. "Hestia, my outburst at your last inquiry into the fate of your parents may have been uncouth, but I hope you now understand that every day your father lived served as a constant reminder of all I had lost, of all that had been taken from me. So, after he and my father passed, I endeavored to create a new life, one where no one lived in the shadow of the great Jonathan Rosewood." The sarcasm dripped from August's tongue like poison, and all three women huddled just a bit closer to each other. August caught this movement and paused, gathering himself. "However, since you are, as you so vehemently remind me, the lady of the house, I suppose it is finally time you know the full, difficult truth. For the deaths of Thaddeus, Jonathan, and Helena Rosewood were unintended consequences to necessary actions. When your father was announced as the heir to the Rosewood legacy, I knew that my fate was sealed. I would reap no benefits, nor enjoy any of the fruits of the labors I had toiled under for so long. Now, I *will* admit that, back then, I had a tendency toward the dramatics when faced with rather upsetting subjects—"

Fidelia let out a snort, which August met with a scowl.

"But never once did I resort to violence. In fact, the day the announcement of your father's succession was made, I deliberately locked myself away in my study to control my temper. And it was in that room that a revelation struck me. That desk that sits in my study had previously belonged to my father. There was one drawer in that desk that I had never opened until that day. And it was in that drawer, on that day, that I discovered my father's journal and learned about my mother. I began to wonder, as I devoured each page of that journal, if the rumors and my father's belief about my mother were true. And if so, if any of her powers had passed to me. So, I called for the servants to bring me the titles that you saw on that bookshelf. I poured over those tomes for the next three days and, sure enough, began to feel the spark of magick course through my veins. Those days were some of the most exciting of my life . . ." August trailed off as he wandered toward the bedchamber's window again. "But even so, I never intended to kill anyone. I simply wished for control, to show both Jonathan and my father that I was not one to be trifled with. But the spell I chose was much too strong."

"The carriage accident," Hestia muttered just loudly enough for August to hear.

"You know this story?"

Hestia nodded and looked toward Fidelia.

August grunted. "I should have known."

"Helena always suspected that you had something to do with Jonathan and Thaddeus' deaths," Fidelia said, shaking her head. "And to think I had allowed myself to give you the benefit of the doubt."

"So, because my grandfather chose to love my father more than he chose to love you, that was just cause for killing them both?" Hestia could feel her ears grow hot as anger slowly began to build within her. "At least I halfway understand your reason for wanting my grandfather dead. But my father—"

"I did not want them dead, Hestia. You must understand that. Besides, you do not know the Jonathan I knew. He was—"

"I did not know my father at all, August! You made sure of that!" Hestia bellowed, addressing August by name for the first time. "You can stand there and claim that you did not mean it and lament that my father stole your father, yet it does not change the fact that you stole my father from me as well. Your father may have rejected you, but at least he lived long enough to do so!" Hestia felt the adrenaline pump through her veins as she stood before a bewildered August.

"I am your uncle, Hestia, and I expect to be addressed as such."

"Technically, you are cousins," Fidelia countered, stepping forward. "At any rate, I would say a confession of murder would eliminate the need for formalities."

August ignored Fidelia's taunting and faced Hestia directly. "It was *fate* that ended your father's life, Hestia. I merely acted as a vehicle."

"And my mother?" Hestia inquired. "You say that this is the room where she took her final breath. Was that the work of *fate* as well?"

"Your mother was a . . . complicated creature. From the moment I saw her, I knew that she was a fierce and intelligent woman that required special care. Care that I never believed your father could provide. But of course, he was blessed with her hand in marriage. Still, I always suspected she knew of my affections. I often caught her stealing glances in my direction when she visited, and even more so after she came to live at the manor. But I never acted on my impulses, knowing that a unique flower such as your mother needed just the right nurturing."

"Hah, my sister told me the stories about your incessant leering," Fidelia interjected. "And she told me of the time when you boldly advanced upon her, gripping her hand as if it already belonged to you. If you ever caught her stealing glances at you, they were surely glances of fear and disgust."

"Yes, well, perhaps my newfound powers at that time had made me a bit . . . presumptuous, but did your dear sister care to mention that she did not remove her hand from mine straight away? Perhaps there was more to Helena than she let on."

Fidelia scowled, fists clenched at her sides. She opened her mouth, prepared for rebuttal, when Hestia broke in.

"If you were so taken with my mother, then how did she come to die under your watch?"

August's gray eyes glassed over, and he lowered his head. "I had every intention of ensuring you and your mother were to be cared for after my father and Jonathan's accident. I wanted us to be a family, and I wanted to give you and Helena everything you needed and desired. I knew that there would be much business to address following the deaths, so I made quick work of the basics. This included hiring a handmaiden who could provide you with proper care while Helena had time to grieve." August nodded toward Jessamine, who flashed Hestia a small smile. "I wanted to arrive home with the promise that Helena would have nothing to concern herself with other than her own emotional recovery. As it was, I barely had the chance to speak, much less make promises, for as soon as I stepped foot in the manor again, your mother charged at me with a barrage of accusations and attacks on my character."

"Sounds like a woman who just wanted the truth," Fidelia remarked.

"What did you say when my mother made these attacks?" Hestia questioned.

"There was little I *could* say," August replied. "So, I allowed her to berate me, hoping that she would get it out of her system, and we could rebuild. Once she finally wore herself out, I had Jessamine lead her back to her chamber and fetch you from your grandparents' home. From that day forward, your mother locked the two of you away in your nursery here, scarcely to be seen until weeks later, when she began to come down for meals. I gave her the time and space she needed, and slowly, she and I began to develop a congenial relationship. It was then when we discussed our future."

Hestia and Fidelia exchanged a look as they suspected the part of the story that was to come.

"After the deaths of my father and Jonathan, all duties, rights, titles, and estates of the Rosewood earldom passed to me, with one exception. Your mother held dower rights to Deston Manor upon Jonathan's demise."

"My mother owned Deston Manor?" Hestia questioned.

August nodded. "Not that she knew the first thing about managing a manor, and certainly one of this size," August said, waving his arms about the chamber. "Which is why I convinced her that the only path forward was for us to marry. This would relieve her of the duties of caring for the manor and further secure her place in society, as well as yours."

Hestia's recurring dream was painfully making more sense. *The white gown. The awning. 'Til death do us part.* A lump formed in her throat as she whispered, "I was there, wasn't I? At the wedding?"

"You were, dearie," Jessamine piped up. "You sat on my lap."

"While it is true that our marriage was in part transactional, there was also a part of me that never lost my affection for Helena. My intuition told me that if she would only spend some time with me, I could give her a more beautiful life than Jonathan ever could."

"I understand that you believe you loved my mother," Hestia said. "Yet, you still haven't answered my first question. If you felt so deeply for her, and longed to give her such a beautiful life, then how did she die in this manor, in this room?"

August let out a deep sigh and turned. Hestia, Fidelia, and Jessamine watched the man closely as he lowered his head. Suddenly, he snapped it upright, as if an idea had sprung into his mind. "It was a Saturday afternoon, one year after my father and Jonathan's deaths and one month after our wedding. I had just arrived home after some business in town, and I recall stepping through the door to an unusually quiet manor. We had never had a large staff, but I was usually greeted by our footman or heard the cook clanging about the kitchen. But there was nothing. I searched the rooms on the first floor and, finding no signs of life, finally made my way to the second floor. I later learned from Jessamine that your mother had excused all of the servants for the day, stating that she wished to be alone with her daughter. It wasn't until I approached the nursery that I knew why." August leaned close to Hestia and placed a hand on her shoulder, as if wishing to now play the part of the loving uncle. "What I am about to tell you will not be easy for you to hear, Hestia, but it is what I saw. As I neared the door to this room, I noticed that it was ajar. I peeked inside and saw you and your mother on the bed. Your mother held a small bottle and a spoon and appeared to be trying to feed you medicine. It was only seconds later when I learned this was no medicine at all."

"What was it?" Hestia asked.

"Arsenic."

CHAPTER FIFTEEN

Tensions erupted in the small chamber room as August's confession approached the ears of all listening parties. Fidelia's face turned red, Hestia's heart raced, and Jessamine's eyes grew wide as saucers.

"That is a lie!" Fidelia was the first to shout. "Say what you will about my sister, but you will not stand there and accuse her of trying to murder her own daughter! That is absolutely ridiculous!"

"I know that you believe you knew your sister better than anyone, but I am only relaying what I saw with my own eyes."

"Why would my mother try to—" the words caught in Hestia's throat as doubt filled her mind.

"My relationship with your mother was not as congenial as she had led me to believe. She was certainly a deft actress, appearing as if she were growing comfortable in her new life, when in reality, her suspicions of my role in the deaths of my father and Jonathan had developed into hysteria." August shook his head. "I know that I am not perfect, but I had promised to treat your mother like the queen she was. She just didn't understand that. Her grief blinded her to everything and made her see only the worst in me. She did not know me, nor did she try. No one has ever seen me for who I am. I am the rightful heir to the Rosewood legacy. I am the man who should have been with Helena. I am—"

"But how does any of that explain why my mother would try to kill me?"

"Your mother thought she was committing an act of mercy. After I swatted the poison from her hands and ushered you out of the room to spare you further harm, she revealed all to me. She felt that killing you and ending her own life was the only recourse to escape the 'fate of being with me,' as she put it. When I asked her to elaborate, she confessed that she had ordered one of the servants to let her into my study while I was away, wherein she discovered those same books you found upon my shelf. According to her, 'Only a man with a truly dark soul would dare to explore such ghastly topics.' She said that she no longer felt that she nor her child were safe in my presence and suspected that I would eventually unleash my wrath upon you both. So, she decided to get out ahead of it and commit you both to the ground herself."

August began to pace the room. "Everything after that moment happened so quickly. I remember seeing a flash as your mother pulled a knife from behind the pillow of her bed. I assume she had grabbed it as a failsafe in case the poison was ineffective. She began brandishing it in my direction, and I held up my hands. Once she saw that I was defenseless, she came to her senses and dropped the weapon. Before she could change her mind, I grabbed her wrists and wrestled her to the ground. Or what I assumed was the ground, for I did not see that, just below Helena, there was a crack in the floorboard. A crack just thick and deep enough to hold a knife upright, its blade pointing skyward. I did not notice any of this until I heard Helena let out a shriek." August's breath suddenly grew shaky. "I had never meant to hurt her. I loved her with all of my soul. She was the last person I wanted to put in harm's way. But she was so . . . reckless at the end. If she hadn't brought that knife upstairs, she may still be alive today. But, as fate would have it, she died in my arms that night, in this very spot." August gestured toward the stained floorboards near the bed.

Hestia leaned down and gently brushed them, as if they held a remnant of her mother's spirit. She examined the spot further as Jessamine chimed in.

"How is it I never knew this story, Lord Rosewood?"

"Well, I was not about to spook the servants with Helena's tragic tale. In fact, I knew it would be best if everything began anew from that moment on. After I dealt with the direct matter of disposing of Helena's corpse and cleaning the room to the best of my ability, I immediately let go of every servant in the manor. Well, every servant except for you, Jessamine. I knew that Hestia would need a mother figure, and you had already grown so close to her. I could not bear to see another woman in my life face such grief. Plus, I knew that I could trust you, a fact that I am proud to say continues to this very night."

Jessamine looked at Hestia, brows furrowed in concern, the young woman still knelt over in the dark, caressing the floor absent-mindedly.

August followed Jessamine's gaze and addressed Hestia directly. "From that day forward, I dedicated my life to ensuring that you received only the best in life, Hestia. I wanted to give you the life that I promised your mother. The life that I wish I'd had when I was your age. And we can still have it." August knelt beside Hestia and wrapped his arm around her. "There is still hope for us, my love. This world has been unkind to us, but we can unite against it. Our marriage will be one of defiance; defiance against a world that has denied us at every turn. I know that I raised you as my niece, but it is my hope that you will see me as an equal and as a partner. Everything I promised your mother will be yours. The date in that book you found is only prospective. I will wait as long as you need to warm up to the idea of our union. But just know that I only wish for what is best for you."

After many moments of staring at the stain in the floorboards, Hestia finally lifted her head and turned toward August with a deadpan expression. "Where is the crack?"

"What?" August asked.

"The crack in the floorboard," Hestia replied, pointing to the spot. "The one you said the knife fell into. Where is it?"

August glanced down at the floorboard in question with a blank look.

"Jessamine, Aunt Delia, do either of you see a crack?"

The two women crept closer and, after looking down at the spot themselves, shook their heads in unison.

"Well, it . . . it's been fixed . . . of course," August stammered.

"Strange, if it were fixed, wouldn't there be new wood here replacing these bloodstained floorboards?" Without waiting for a reply, Hestia began to pace about the room, touching every surface she passed. "It's funny how the mind works, isn't it? How memories can lay dormant for so long, only to rush back at a given moment."

"Hestia?" August asked.

She merely flashed him a sly grin. "I was about three years old when all of this occurred, correct?"

"Hestia–"

"August."

The lord's eyes thinned into slits. "Yes, I believe you were about three years old."

"Old enough to begin developing memories. So, please tell me, August, because you say you ushered me out of the room following your discovery of me and my mother, why then did seeing that spot on the floorboards and hearing your story suddenly trigger a memory so unlike the story you just shared?"

One could cut the tension with a knife as Fidelia and Jessamine exchanged glances. August's eyes remained trained on Hestia, who returned the favor, a hint of glee making them sparkle in the dimly lit room.

"I have had this recurring dream for months now. It always begins the same. A man and a woman stand beneath an awning of white roses. The man grabs the woman's wrists, and she tries to break free. But then, her white dress turns crimson, and she screams as the man says, 'Til death do us part.' Then, a door locks them away. The door to this very room, as I now know. All the time I have tried to understand what this dream could mean, what it could possibly be trying to tell me. But then you brought me into this room tonight, and you showed me the stain in the floorboards, and you regaled us all with your valiant attempt at a tale of tragic loss, and I remembered. That dream was never a dream at all, it was a memory. A memory that I never knew I possessed until tonight. And one that I am sure you never knew I possessed at all."

August's eyes grew wide.

"What do you remember, Hestia?" Fidelia asked.

"August did get a few things right in his story. It *did* take place in this room, and there *was* a knife. But there was no poison. My mother didn't try to kill me. She was packing so we could run away."

August began breathing sharply through his nose as Hestia continued.

"The piece that I don't believe you know, August, is that my mother had told me to grab my doll from the hallway as she continued to pack. When I returned a moment later, I saw you in the room with her."

"And what did you see next, Hestia?" August's voice had taken on a menacing tone at this point that sent shivers down Jessamine and Fidelia's spines.

"Not much, admittedly, as I could only peek through the cracked door. But I heard you plead with her to stay, and I heard her reject you. I also heard her admit that your marriage was illegitimate as she never signed the certificate. She still owned Deston Manor and intended to sell it as soon as she escaped your grasp."

"That certainly sounds more like the sister I knew," Fidelia smugly said.

"Anything else, Hestia?" August's face was still as stone.

"I heard some shuffling, some banging, and saw a flash of a knife. And then I heard my mother ... scream." Hestia paused as the pain of the memory enveloped her for a moment. "And then I heard you speak five words, the same I heard so many times in my dream ..."

"'Til death do us part." Both Hestia and August uttered the last words in unison.

Hestia looked up at August in anger. "My mother's death was not accidental. You *killed* her, just like you killed my father. You killed her because she was one more person in your life who saw the true evil in you and wished to run away from it. If anyone ever tried to poison me in my life, it was *you*. You tried to poison me against my own family by keeping me in the dark for so long and by making up such ridiculous lies when forced to bring things to light. And then to have the audacity to plan to marry me, and to what? Fulfill some sick fantasy you never could with my mother? To what end? So, I could try to run away and meet the same fate? I must say, August, I am glad that you left the manor those few days ago. For if you hadn't, the course of events would not have unfolded to lead me to the truth I knew all along. You are no uncle, lord, or even a man. You are a monster."

The room grew silent as Hestia's final words dissipated like smoke. Jessamine's face held a look of shock, while Fidelia's beamed with pride. August, on the other hand, slowly lowered his head and turned away from the women. He remained in this manner for several minutes as Hestia, Fidelia, and Jessamine exchanged glances. The three stared at the dark form before them as August's shoulders began to move up and down. It took them a moment, but they finally heard the faint sound of giggling.

"I've been found out," August squeaked out between bursts of laughter. "You are right, Hestia. I am a monster. I suppose there is nothing left to do but what a monster like me does best." At that moment, August turned around and the dim light of the room bounced off of the shiny head of a pistol in his left hand. "I must destroy."

CHAPTER SIXTEEN

Panic burst through the chamber room in waves. August, now with a maniacal glint in his eyes, shifted the barrel of the pistol back and forth between Hestia and Fidelia.

"Lord Rosewood, please think of what you are doing here." Jessamine jumped in front of Hestia, hoping to diffuse things.

"Oh, trust me, Jessamine, I *have* thought of what I am doing. I thought about it the entire way home after hearing from you. I tried reasoning, and I tried appealing to Hestia's delicate nature by softening the blow of her mother's death." August turned his body, pistol included, toward Fidelia with a grimace. "None of this would have happened if *you* hadn't come here, but you just *had* to worm your way into my manor."

"What are you going to do, August? Kill me? Like you killed my sister? Like you killed Jonathan? Well, go ahead, I am here before you. Show us firsthand who you truly are!" Fidelia now stood mere inches away from August's face, her chest pushed into the end of the pistol. She stared August down as his mouth twitched in anger.

"You Ward women have always been trouble. I could tell that from the first day we met all those years ago. If your sister had just taken the time to know me, she would have fallen in love with me first. I would have given her a life most women only dream about. But, perhaps killing her was a good thing. After all, what's one less willful, disrespectful, disobedient woman in the world?"

August twisted the butt of the pistol into Fidelia's chest as he spoke these last lines.

"I—I trusted you, Lord Rosewood," Jessamine stammered. "All these years. When you said that Lady Rosewood's death was a tragic accident, I believed you. I thought you were a good man. That's why when I heard Ms. Evans . . . or whoever she is . . . filling Hestia's head with what I believed to be wild stories, I tried to warn you."

"Your loyalty has not gone unnoticed, Jessamine," August replied. "You will be rewarded handsomely for your work in tonight's events."

"I quit."

August's head snapped in Jessamine's direction. "Excuse me?"

"You heard me, Lord Rosewood. I said I quit. When you hired me, it was to see to the wellbeing of that young girl." Jessamine pointed at Hestia. "Well, that girl is a young woman now, so it seems my work here is finished. I am sorry, sir, but I cannot in good conscience continue working for a man who I now know to be a murderer."

August let out a long sigh. "Oh, Jessamine. You know, I really liked you. I was even going to let you live as a reward for helping me. But if I let you quit, who's to say you won't turn me into the authorities?" August removed his pistol from Fidelia's chest and pointed it directly at Jessamine, who held up her hands. "I am sorry, but I'm afraid I am going to have to *let you go*."

What occurred next took seconds, but Hestia swore that time stood still. August pulled the trigger of his pistol, and a bullet shot out with a loud *bang*. Hestia turned to Jessamine, who stood just long enough to display a small hole in her forehead before crumpling to the ground with a *thud*. Hestia and Fidelia stood in utter shock before Hestia raced toward the handmaiden. "Jessamine, Jessamine, Jessamine!" She cradled Jessamine's head in her lap, blood staining her hands and the skirt of her dress. She watched the cheery brown eyes that greeted her every morning slowly turn white and the rosy tint of her cheeks drain of all color. And for the very first time that evening, every pent-up emotion released itself as tears began streaming down Hestia's face, her body erupting in convulsions.

Fidelia rushed to her niece's side, placing a gentle hand on her shoulder.

August only stared blankly at Jessamine's lifeless form, as if dissociating completely from the man he once was. Or rather, accepting the man he had always been. "We can still be a family, Hestia," August finally choked out in a moment of clarity. "I will give you one final chance. Accept me as I am, and no one else will be hurt tonight."

Hestia halted her tremors just long enough to look up at August with darkened eyes. "H-how, a-after all of this, c-could you possibly think that I would want anything to do with you?" As her voice evened out and her breathing returned to normal, she gently placed Jessamine's head on the floor and rose to face August. Throwing all caution to the wind, she stomped toward him until their faces were inches apart. She leaned in, and spat, "August Rosewood, the only time I will accept you as you are is when you are dead."

August stared at Hestia, both refusing to break eye contact. Finally, he sighed and backed away, holding up his hands in defeat. "Fine. If you do not wish to be with me, then I will not force you to stay. The truth is, I am tired of having to threaten those I love to love me back. So, go. Go with your aunt and turn me in. I am ready to face the justice I deserve."

Hestia and Fidelia exchanged anxious glances. August had just shot Jessamine at the possibility of her turning him in. Now, he was telling them to go and do the same?

Testing the waters, Fidelia grabbed Hestia's arm and began leading her toward the door. "Come, Hestia. We should go."

Hestia continued to stare at August before turning to face the bedchamber's exit. The two women just reached the threshold when they heard August whisper something incoherent.

"What was that?" Fidelia questioned, turning around.

"I said, say hello to your sister for me." Another bullet released from August's pistol, and just as before, pierced straight through Fidelia's forehead.

Blood spattered across Hestia's face as the woman fell to the floor in a heap. A sharp scream filled the air as Hestia fell apart.

August, on the other hand, calmly walked over to the scene and surveyed his work carefully. As Hestia burst into hysterical cries, he smirked with glee. "Such a foolish girl, to think I would actually let you leave so easily. A true lady of the house would never behave with such naivete. But don't worry, my darling, you have all the time in the world to learn. For, you see, Hestia, I am going to get what I want for once. And no one is going to stop me."

Hestia's cries cut out as she faced August, this time, being the one to let out a sigh of defeat. "Fine. Y-you win. I will stay here with you."

"You will?" With a smile, August wrapped his arms around Hestia.

The girl's arms remained at her sides for a moment until she noticed a flash of light bounce off of the pistol in August's hand. Hestia wriggled her arms free, feigning a return of August's affection, but instead of embracing him, she reached her hand toward the one that held the pistol and, finding a tender spot of flesh, pinched it with her fingers.

August yelped and released the pistol.

Hestia caught it just before it hit the ground and marveled, only for a brief moment, at how surprisingly light it felt in her hand. Was the weight of death so insignificant, or was it August's in particular that made her next moves feel almost natural? Hestia slowly pointed the barrel of the pistol between August's eyes.

He smiled and knelt to the ground, a small chuckle rising in his throat. "Are you going to kill me, Hestia?" August asked calmly. "Perhaps you and I are more alike than I ever thought possible."

Hestia placed her index finger upon the trigger, and August closed his eyes. Just as she was about to pull, she felt a soft, cold hand reach across her own.

"You cannot do this, Hestia."

August's eyes snapped open as Hestia's own followed the hand to a figure that stood on her left. It took a moment in the dim light of the room, but she finally made out an all too familiar face and gasped. "Adella?" Hestia questioned.

"Yes, and I must implore you not to kill my son."

CHAPTER SEVENTEEN

Adella guided Hestia's arm, lowering the weapon until it fell from the young woman's hand and clanked upon the wooden floor. Hestia's eyes shifted from Adella to August, the latter of whom rose from his knees.

"How are you speaking?" August inquired. "That spell was to last—"

"Only until you returned home," Adella interjected. "Well, you have returned, and so has my voice."

"I–I don't understand," Hestia broke in. "Did you say that August is your—?"

"I apologize, Hestia, for burdening you with one more revelation on what I am sure has already been a harrowing night."

"B-but how?" Hestia stammered. "You look so—"

"Well, I have picked up a few beauty secrets in my time." Adella popped a small bottle out of her pocket that contained an unknown liquid and some herbs.

"So, it *is* true," Hestia began. "You are a . . ."

"Witch, yes. We both are." Adella gestured toward August, who still stood a few feet away. At that moment, her eyes caught the lifeless figures that lay on the floor behind her son. "Not again," Adella whispered, rushing to and kneeling beside Jessamine and Fidelia. She snapped her head at August, brows furrowed in anger. "When will it be enough, August? When will there be enough blood on your hands for you to realize that your lot in life is your own undoing?"

August snorted. "That is rich coming from a curse con-jurer like you. What is the meaning of this intrusion anyhow? You have succeeded in keeping Hestia from killing me. What more do you desire?"

"I *first* desire you to keep your mouth shut," Adella rose up, her index finger pointing directly at August's chest. "I dare say you have done quite enough tonight."

"What does he mean by 'curse conjurer,' Adella?"

The maid looked at Hestia, her gaze immediately soften-ing. She stepped toward the girl, taking up her hands. "Hestia, I am sure you have heard enough tales tonight to make your head spin, so I hope you have the energy to indulge me in one more. I will warn you, though, that after this account, you may view me differently. In which case, I will completely understand." Adella let out a sigh, as if preparing to bare her soul, before launching into her story.

"As a witch, I was born with a gift of second sight. I could see events that had not yet transpired. It was a wholly imperfect gift at first; I had no control over when the visions would come, nor any knowledge of how far in the future they would ultimately take place. Some visions were hazy, like looking through a dense fog. Others, as clear as if they were my own thoughts. I eventually learned to hone this gift, but not before my young and fickle heart met Thaddeus Rosewood. From the moment I set my eyes upon him, I fell head over heels. I was so foolishly convinced that our connection was fated, even when I knew his heart to belong to another at the time. I had somehow convinced myself that he would eventually realize that he was meant to be with me, and we would live together in happiness. Now, I am sure that August has told you enough to know that I did not receive the happy ending I had so desired. When Thaddeus rejected me in favor of the woman he truly loved, I fell into such a hole of grief that quickly devolved into blind rage. It was in this rage and this heartbreak that I cast a curse. I wanted Thaddeus to feel the same pain, the same heartbreak, that I felt. However, in my rampage, I had neglected to set limits on the curse. It wasn't until I heard about the death of his love that I suspected my wrongdoing. And shortly after that event, I discovered that I was pregnant."

Adella gestured to August, who shook his head in disgust. "My mother disowned me as soon as she learned that I was pregnant with Thaddeus' child, and I was thrown penniless into the street. I tried to create a life of my own after that, but once August was born, things grew tougher, and I could barely take care of myself, much less a child. It was then that I made the difficult decision to leave him at his father's doorstep. At that time, I did not suspect that my curse had encapsulated *all* manners of love, including familial, or I wouldn't have dared to leave him with Thaddeus, for fear he would have been marked. I thought I was giving him his best chance at the life he deserved."

August snorted. "Best chance? You left me with a neglectful tyrant!"

Adella flashed August a stern look that faded to one of longing. "Perhaps if you had stayed with *me*, I could have prevented . . ." the maid's voice choked as she glanced about the room.

"Is that why you are here now, Adella? To help August contend with your curse?" Hestia questioned.

"Well, to be honest, I am here in large part because of you, Hestia. Though I had left my only child, I never strayed too far from Deston. I lived on the streets of London, begging and peddling whatever I could to achieve some level of social standing. I also used what little free time I had to strengthen my gifts, and even spent time working as a fortune teller for those in the upper classes who found enjoyment in the metaphysical arts. Even as I began to sharpen my second sight, I still could not quite control it, nor could I conjure any visions of my son. I later learned that he was inadvertently blocking me with his own powers, so I had to rely on news and idle gossip when I came across it. That was how I had heard of your parents' marriage, your birth, and the announcement of your father's future appointment as the next earl of the Rosewood family." Adella paused and looked over at

August. "When I heard that last announcement, something in my bones told me that August, if he was anything like his mother, wouldn't take such a betrayal lightly. However, against my better judgment, I waited. I waited and hoped. There was really nothing more I *could* do. And for a while, afterward, all seemed well. Then, came that one night. I was awoken from a dead sleep by the most powerful vision I had ever encountered. There was so much pain and fear behind it that even thinking of it now sends a chill up my spine."

"What did you see?" Hestia asked.

"I saw a great carriage fall over a cliffside, carrying two terrified men inside. The younger man I did not recognize, but there was no mistaking the older man who joined him. It was Thaddeus Rosewood himself."

"My father and grandfather."

"Yes," Adella responded. "I later learned this vision occurred only twenty-four hours prior to their deaths, and the pit in my stomach that followed that vision still haunts me to this day. For it was then that the revelation struck regarding the subjects of my curse. Up until that point, the only person whose death I suspected had been a result of my curse was the woman that Thaddeus had been in love with. From that, I had unwisely assumed that it only impacted the subjects of *romantic* love. However, Thaddeus' love for your father, as evidenced by his appointment, had marked poor Jonathan for death." Adella paused and placed a hand upon Hestia's shoulder. "I chastise myself every day for playing a part in such tragedy, Hestia. I will never forgive myself."

Hestia shook Adella's hand off of her shoulder. "So, my father's death was to be inevitable regardless of August's hand? For the simple reason that he was loved by my grandfather?"

"Yes," Adella responded.

"Well, when Thaddeus also died in that carriage crash, did that break the curse?"

"I thought it had, until I had my second vision, sometime later. It came to me again in the middle of the night. I saw a woman with long, blonde hair. I heard her screams. I smelled the must of the bedchamber's air. And I witnessed, as clearly as if I had been there, the man responsible for taking this woman's last breath. Though he was fully grown, none of my instincts could deny who he was. For the first time, I was looking at my own son, August Rosewood."

"My mother's death," Hestia said.

Adella nodded, her face full of sorrow. "That familiar pit in my stomach returned that night, and with it, another revelation. For something in my soul told me that your mother's impending death was also the result of my curse, but logic fought that Thaddeus was dead, and the curse was no more. It wasn't until I gave it more thought that I realized my curse must have spread, so all who bore the blood of Thaddeus Rosewood would carry this curse in their veins. My son was never at risk of being marked, but rather, was doomed to mark a love of his own."

"What did you do next, Adella?"

"Well, hoping that I still had time to prevent this act before it was carried out, I set out for Deston Manor that very night. Unfortunately, a brutal storm began tearing through the area shortly after I began my journey. I fought with every ounce of strength I possessed to endure it, but even my most powerful health spells were no match for the wind, rain, and fog that seeped into my skin and disoriented my mind. I became lost, and eventually, succumbed to illness, falling into an unconsciousness that I did not wake from for nearly one week. When I finally returned to myself, I was in Deston, and the act I had set out to prevent had long been accomplished." Adella paused as the pain of her memories returned to her. "Once I regained my strength, I endeavored to visit Deston Manor anyway to reconnect with my child and perhaps prevent any future suffering. So, with nothing more than the clothes upon my back, I made the final trek to the manor, and at last, reunited with my son."

"What did August do when he saw you?"

"He threatened to call the authorities, of course."

"What would *you* do if a strange woman arrived at your door proclaiming to be your long-lost mother?" August interjected.

"Yes, it took a bit of convincing before August accepted the truth of who I was," Adella said. "But, when I told him of my visions and of the curse and its implications, his countenance seemed to change. He suddenly appeared before me in an almost child-like state and laid bare all he had endured since I had left him with Thaddeus. If my son holds any talent, it is surely one for storytelling. He had me so enraptured that I actually began to feel empathy for him, even as he confessed to his direct roles in the deaths of Thaddeus, Jonathan, and Helena. I knew that, both legally and to protect anyone else from harm, he would have to be turned into the proper authorities. But I couldn't help but feel my own sense of responsibility for the events that had transpired. I assured August that I would support him, and we could both use our gifts to try to find a way to break the curse. However, the events that followed later that night eradicated all warmth I held for him for good."

"What happened?"

Adella turned and bore her eyes directly into her son's skull. "August had agreed to my help and to turn himself in but convinced me to spend one night in the manor, promising we would address everything in the morning. While I slept in the room across from him, he bound my magick and tied me indelibly to Deston Manor. Any attempts I made to leave would be met with a burning pain so great that every nerve in my body would feel like it was on fire. He condemned me indefinitely, and it was then that I truly learned of the man my son had become."

"You abandoned me for years, and then upon our first meeting, you wished for me to turn myself into the authorities? I simply did what any man in my situation would have done," August stated.

"Oh, August, the curse I cast may have doomed so many to death, but you cursed yourself by allowing your jealousy and rage to lead you to murder. And it hasn't stopped, as evidenced by tonight's activities. That beast that lives inside of you is one of your own design. Nothing will change that the son I brought into this world is, and forever will be, a demon among men." August smirked as Adella continued. "And that is why tonight's events have occurred. My purpose was never to save you, August, nor was it to save those we have lost. Rather, it has always been to set into motion the series of events that would save that poor girl." Adella pointed at Hestia and then folded her arms smugly. "Thank goodness I had finally undone those binding spells you cast upon me."

"Undone them?" August questioned.

"Did you really think I would be willingly held captive as your servant for the rest of my days?" She let out a short chuckle before turning back to Hestia. "It wasn't easy, as moments of solitude as a maid are difficult to come by, but eventually, I had practiced enough to break the binds and regain my powers. It was then that my visions also returned, and I discovered that you would one day hold feelings for Hestia and mark her for the same fate that befell her parents. And all that time, I played the role of quiet and dutiful servant, reluctantly bowing to your every whim and following your strict orders to never be found in Hestia's presence."

"Because you knew too much," Hestia stated.

Adella nodded. "That was perhaps the hardest part of my plan, having to watch you grow up from afar knowing all that I knew. There were so many things I wanted to tell you, even during times as recent as when we ran into each other in the hallway those few days ago, shortly before August took my voice. Still, even then, I knew that speech wasn't the only way to communicate. That night we met in the hall, you spoke of a recurring dream. And I am sure you know now that dream was a culmination of your memories. But did it ever strike you as odd that they began occurring seemingly out of the blue?"

"I suppose," Hestia said, eyeing Adella curiously. The witch just flashed her a small smile and Hestia's eyes grew wide. "That was *you*." Hestia's brows furrowed as other memories came into question. "Aunt Delia mentioned that she had the same dream, and that her sleepwalking returned suddenly after arriving at the manor. Was that—?"

"Also, me," Adella said.

Suddenly, it was as if multiple locks unlatched themselves within Hestia's mind. The young woman thought back to her conversation with Adella that night before everything began. She thought about her dreams, about Fidelia's dream. She thought about her first meeting with Ezekiel when he said that Adella had pointed at her door. "It's *always* been you."

Adella smiled. "Everything had to be carefully calculated so things could be gently nudged into the proper place. Some of it was magickal intervention, like with your dreams. Some of it was mundane, like convincing August that you needed a new governess and dropping parchments off in an alley outside of your aunt's workhouse."

Hestia recalled Fidelia's story about the strange figure she saw who left the ads that led her to become Hestia's new governess. Her emotions reeled as each revelation snapped into place within her like pieces of a jigsaw puzzle that she never even knew had been incomplete. In a fit of emotion, she flung her arms around the witch's shoulders, who returned the embrace.

"I am sorry for all that you have suffered, Hestia," Adella whispered. "It was never my intention to have such innocent blood on my hands. No one should have to bear witness to all that you have endured, and for that, I will never forgive myself." Adella pulled away from Hestia's embrace and grabbed her shoulders tightly. "But now is the time for me to pay my penance and try to make at least one thing right. Hestia, I want you to run to the gardener's cottage. Ezekiel has come into your life for a reason, and he and his father will help you escape. Leave Deston Manor, and run as far away as you can. Start a new life away from all of this. You are free, so please do not take this opportunity in vain."

"Adella, I cannot—"

"Hestia, I have sired evil into this world. Please let me be the one to remove it." With that, Adella slowly lowered herself and picked up the pistol that still lay upon the cold floor. She rose back up and raised the pistol toward August's head.

August let out a maniacal chuckle. "Oh, this is just too perfect. Mother, you and I both know that you will never pull that trigger. As much as you'd like to believe you have what it takes to end my life, you will falter when it matters most. You are not the first person who has wanted me dead, and you will not be the last. But your life will end just like all the others: with the knowledge that I still go on and will always go on, from now until the end—"

August's speech was cut short as a loud bang echoed through the bedchamber. The lord's eyes grew wide as he looked down at his chest, where a small hole had been ripped in the dead-center of his jacket. His head turned upward just long enough to flash his eyes at Adella before he fell to the floor.

"Oh my God," Hestia whispered.

"Hestia, go," Adella urged.

"But Adella—"

"*Now!*"

Quickly, Hestia ran out the door of the nursery. Without once looking back, the girl raced down the stairs of the dark manor and sprinted toward the main doors, throwing them open and allowing the cool summer air to hit her skin. Just before she crossed the threshold, she looked behind her into the black expanse of the place she had known as her home for fifteen years. While Deston Manor once felt claustrophobic, it now felt sad and empty. Goosebumps prickled Hestia's arms as she tried to catch her breath. Finally, gathering her resolve, Hestia set foot beyond the manor's doors and raced out into the moonlight, making her way toward Ezekiel's cottage.

Meanwhile, Adella stared at her son with the pistol still pointed, who lay bleeding on the bedchamber floor. August's blood pooled beneath him, spreading across the stain that had already tasted blood once before. She watched the body carefully, alert to any potential retaliatory movements. Suddenly, she heard a weak voice call out.

"M–mother."

Despite all he had put her through, instinct took over as Adella raced over to her dying child. She picked up August's head and cradled it in her lap, running her hands across his face as if to soothe him from a nightmare. "In spite of everything, you are and always will be my son. I love you," Adella whispered. "Perhaps that is my true curse." She held tighter onto her son, not wanting him to feel alone as his life drained from his body.

Just before he left completely, August slowly jerked his hand up, as if intent to give his mother one final embrace. Instead, he used his last bit of strength to wrench the pistol from Adella's hand. Shaking, he aimed the pistol toward his mother, who watched him carefully before closing her eyes. Her face softened as a sense of peace, one she had not felt in a very long time, finally washed over her.

A single gunshot rang out through the expansive halls of Deston Manor before turning silent—as silent, and still, and black as death itself.

CHAPTER EIGHTEEN

Ezekiel Miller tossed and turned in his bed. While he usually slept fitfully, this night was particularly difficult as dark dreams plagued his mind. He saw himself and Hestia standing under what appeared to be an altar. As he took her hands in his own, he noticed that they felt unusually cold. He looked up at Hestia's face, only to be met with two round, black voids where her eyes should have been. Her skin appeared gaunt, every bone visible through paper-thin flesh.

"Why did you have to—" Hestia began, only to be cut off by a cascade of blood running out of her mouth.

Ezekiel screamed as Hestia continued to choke until she fell at his feet.

The boy shot up in his bed, out of breath and dripping in sweat. He frantically looked around but saw nothing more than the dark outline of his father's sleeping figure and the simple surroundings of his family's cottage. Ezekiel allowed his breathing to return to normal and prepared to lay back down when he heard a small rapping at the door. *Who would be calling on us at this hour?* Ezekiel thought. Gingerly, he tiptoed out of his bed and made his way to the door. He opened it, being met with a sight that nearly made him faint.

Hestia Rosewood stood before him, her fair blonde hair in a tangle. Her already porcelain skin appeared even whiter, as if all of the blood had left her body. Her green eyes appeared puffy and red, and a large dark stain adorned her skirts.

"Hestia!" Ezekiel exclaimed, throwing the door open completely. "What on earth—?"

Before he could form another word, Hestia threw her arms around him and gripped him tightly, bursting into a sudden fit of tears. The gardener's boy held the young lady as shakes began to wrack her body. A sudden surge of protectiveness ran through him as he pulled her closer and looked behind her for any other signs of life.

"'Zkiel," Ambrose muttered from within the cottage as Hestia's cries stirred him from his slumber. "'Zkiel, what is going on?"

"It's Lady Rosewood, father," Ezekiel replied, still holding the aforementioned girl in his arms. "I think something serious has happened at the manor."

Ambrose rose fully from his bed and examined the sight before him. He saw Ezekiel standing at the doorway with Hestia fully encased in his arms. Even with only the dim light of the moon to assist him, he could make out the same stain that Ezekiel noticed upon her skirts and jumped up to light the lamps. "Well, don't just stand there with her, boy, bring 'er in."

Ezekiel shuffled a still-crying Hestia into the cottage and sat her down at their dining table. She worked to compose herself, her cries dying down to mere sniffles. Ezekiel and Ambrose watched her intently until they felt she was finally able to speak. "What happened, Lady Rosewood?" Ambrose questioned.

Hestia looked from Ezekiel to Ambrose and let out a long sigh. Her voice still shaking, she began the retelling of the events that transpired over the last couple days. As her tale concluded with her arrival at their cottage, father and son sat back in their chairs in bewilderment.

"Well, I, uh—I'm not too sure I have the words, to be honest," Ambrose finally chimed in.

"Adella told me to run away from Deston Manor and to never look back. She also told me to come here, that you both would help me."

"We have to help Hestia, father," Ezekiel said.

"We can't just leave our post, son. We have a responsibility to the manor."

"Father, if what Hestia is saying is true, and I have no doubt believing it is, there is no longer a lord or a family to serve at this manor. Lord Rosewood is . . . dead, and Hestia cannot stay here."

Hestia flashed Ezekiel an appreciative smile.

"Well, we can't just leave in the middle of the night. Not if there are bodies up there like she says. The second the authorities find 'em and know that we ran, they are going to suspect us. And they won't stop until they've found us."

"I suppose we should alert the authorities, then," Ezekiel said. The boy rose from his seat and grabbed his shoes as Hestia stared out the window at the dark manor that loomed in the distance.

"I can't go to another relative," Hestia whispered. "I don't even know if there are other Rosewoods left."

Ezekiel caught this and gave Hestia a compassionate look. "Maybe the authorities don't have to know that you're here. We can tell them that you ran away before the deaths happened."

"And then what is she supposed to do?" Ambrose questioned.

"Well, then she can run away with us. It couldn't hurt to have an extra person around, right?"

"Well, I suppose that'd be alright. Might be nice to have a lady around again."

"In that case, before I go find the constable, why don't we head back up to the manor to get you some fresh clothes?" Ezekiel pointed to the blood stain on Hestia's skirt.

"I don't know if I can go back in there," Hestia said.

"I will be there with you every step of the way." Ezekiel took up Hestia's hand in his own and gave it a reassuring squeeze. "We'll be back, father."

With that, the pair stepped out the cottage door and into the night, heading toward the manor. Once they reached the door, Hestia turned to face Ezekiel. "Thank you, Ezekiel. You have sacrificed so much for me, and I don't know how I will ever repay you."

"It's my pleasure, Hestia. Now, go, I will be right here when you come back out."

Hestia turned to open the door but suddenly spun back and placed her lips upon Ezekiel's. The boy stood shocked for a moment before wrapping his arms around her and eagerly returning the kiss.

The couple broke a moment later, and Hestia disappeared into the blackness of the manor. She did not allow herself to think as she raced toward her bedchamber. Once inside, she collected a new outfit and a couple of her favorite books. As she ran back out, items in hand, a sudden thought stopped her. She placed her clothes and books down in the hall and scuttled to the room that had been her aunt's sleeping quarters. She scrambled in the dark, desperate to find what she was looking for. She sighed in defeat until she recalled another place the item she sought may be. Gulping, she gingerly made her way down the hall and toward the staircase that led to the second floor. Each step seemed to echo in the deep silence of the manor, as if the walls themselves had died along with everyone within them. As Hestia made it upstairs and stalked down the hallway, she could hear her own heartbeat in her ears.

Finally, she made it to the open bedchamber and made a beeline for her aunt's body. She leaned down and rummaged through the pockets of Fidelia's dress until her hand caught a square piece of paper. She pulled it out and came face to face with the photo of her mother and aunt. Hestia looked from the photo to Fidelia, who lay cold and motionless. "I love you, Aunt Delia." She leaned down and kissed her aunt's forehead before rising to her feet.

Before she left, she willed herself to look around the rest of the bedchamber. She saw the silhouette of Jessamine's body, laying just a foot away from her aunt's. She also caught sight of August, his body as still and rigid as she had ever seen. But one body was missing from the sad troop. *Where's Adella?*

The thought struck Hestia like lightning and sent a chill up her spine. She peered around the room, looked into the hallway, and silently stood, as if awaiting some sign of life. But when none came, she resolved that Adella must have somehow escaped August's gunshot and run off, though to where she may never know. Upon this assumption, Hestia tucked her aunt's photograph away, raced down the stairs, grabbed her clothes and books, and threw the main doors to Deston Manor open, revealing Ezekiel.

The two trotted back to the cottage, and Hestia went inside while Ezekiel made the trek into town to alert the constable.

The next twenty-four hours were a blur as Hestia hid while Ezekiel and Ambrose filed their report. They wove a tale of jealousy, rage, and murder, all with August at the helm. It wasn't entirely untrue, but they did choose to eliminate mentions of the curse and any black magick workings that may have been involved. Hestia's heart also welled with appreciation when she heard Ezekiel tell the constable that Hestia had run off. Then, there was the matter of allowing the undertaker to collect the bodies, informing Hiram that his post as cook was no longer required, and cleaning up all of the final details to close out the case of the Rosewood Murders.

Finally, after about a week, Hestia, Ezekiel, and Ambrose were finally free to pack up and leave the cursed land of the manor behind. As Hestia helped to pack the last trunk, a wide smile crossed her lips that made Ezekiel raise an eyebrow.

"What's got you in such a good mood?"

"I think I just feel . . . happy. For the first time since I cannot even recall."

Ezekiel smiled back at Hestia and the two leaned forward and shared another brief kiss. As they pulled away, Hestia looked deeply into Ezekiel's eyes. *Intense gray eyes,* Hestia thought. *They seem so . . . familiar.* Hestia's face dropped for a second.

"Is there something wrong, Hestia?"

"No," Hestia replied, shaking her head. "No, nothing at all."

"Come on, you two! We better be on our way!" Ambrose shouted from outside the cottage.

Ezekiel and Hestia followed his voice through the window and found him sitting atop of the carriage that once belonged to August. The two gathered the remaining trunks and ran outside to meet him.

"I didn't know you could drive a carriage, Mr. Miller," Hestia said, climbing into the carriage as Ezekiel packed the last trunk in the back.

"A jack of many trades, I am, dearie."

A small lump formed in Hestia's throat as she was suddenly reminded of Jessamine.

Ezekiel followed Hestia into the carriage's passenger compartment, and she placed her head upon his shoulder and closed her eyes. So quickly did Hestia fall into her first restful sleep in ages, and so eagerly was the group looking ahead, that they neglected to see a figure in the distance behind them, waving its arms wildly. If only they had known the danger this figure sought to profess as they were carried away from the House of Rosewood and into an uncertain future.

ACKNOWLEDGMENTS

This book would not exist without the support of the following people:

My beta readers, Shanna Westfall, Kelly Giegierich, and James Grealis – Your insights and enthusiasm at the earliest stage of this process helped guide this project to where it stands today. I am most grateful for your support and look forward to picking your brains on the next adventure.

My editor, Mozelle Jordan – Even the most seasoned writer knows that we can all benefit from another set of eyes, but that's often easier said than done when your manuscript is like your child. I am so appreciative of the care, detail, and patience you invested into this process (and for bringing to light my apparent love of repetitious phrases). Here's to many more projects together!

My 12th grade Creative Writing teacher, Rebecca Hicks – Your class was the incubator for the very first iteration of what would eventually become this novella. Thank you for fostering that creative spark.

And, of course, I cannot leave this page without acknowledging the two most important people who have helped me in my journey – my parents, Chuck and Carrie Hawley. You both have shaped me into the person and writer that I am today. You have read every story I've written about my twisted Rosewood family (even the ones that will never see the light of day!), supported me every step of the way, and never let me give up on my dream. You showed me love (yes, even of the "tough" variety) when I needed it the most, and it is because of you that this book is being read today.

From the bottom of my heart, thank you, thank you, thank you.